MW01204270

CORNSTALKED

Beware of Nebraska cornfields, they can be murder!

PATRICIA BREMMER

Patricia A. Bremmer

Cornstalked

Copyright © 2011

Patricia Bremmer

Second Printing
August 2011

13 digit ISBN   978-0-9845934-3-9

For additional copies contact:
www.windcallenterprises.com

Cover photo: Martin Bremmer

Printed in the USA

www.patriciabremmer.com

This book is dedicated to my daughter, Dawn.

CHAPTER 1

The agonizing decision to phone the Perkins County Sheriff's office was reached after a long, worrisome night for Kimberly Clarke. Her dark brown eyes, noticeably bloodshot, burned and ached as she searched the Internet for the phone number. Her hand trembled as her fingers struggled to maintain her grip on the pen while she scribbled on the personalized notepad—*From the Desk of Bruce Clarke.*

Glancing back toward the computer to be certain she transposed the numbers correctly, she strained to read the screen blurring in and out of focus. Placing the pen on the desk, she raised her clenched fists to her eyes and rubbed vigorously, applying the most pressure to the inner corners. Moisture surfaced, soothing her dry eyes. She checked the phone number again.

Bruce had neglected to provide his wife with a complete itinerary for his hunting trip. His final destination was kept private while the time to expect him home was the only information he felt necessary to share. By contrast, Kimberly obediently made available to him her daily schedule, broken into hourly segments, just as he demanded.

While studying a map of Nebraska to choose the perfect spot for his annual pheasant hunt, Grant, Nebraska, near the state line between Colorado and Nebraska, caught Bruce's attention. He was intrigued with the name, Grant. Being a banker, the word reminded him of money—a government grant, per se. Bruce told Kimberly he felt assured he would be *granted* his limit of birds if he hunted that area—a sort of omen describing his hunting success.

Without that snippet of conversation, she'd have been at a loss as to where to call for assistance. At least she knew that a place named Grant, Nebraska existed, and with the help of the Internet, she learned it was located in Perkins County. Extending her search provided her with the phone number for the sheriff's department.

When Bruce failed to check in with her the night before, that all- to-familiar fear and panic slowly crept in. Not once during their ten-year relationship had he missed the opportunity to catch her somewhere she shouldn't be or doing something she shouldn't be doing, according to his rules. Fortunately, for Kimberly, that opportunity never materialized.

She always went out of her way to avoid a conflict with him. Her life remained an open book for him to examine at will.

When Bruce relinquished that control over her last evening, especially when he was expecting an important phone call, she had to wonder what could have prevented him from contacting her.

That business call, destined to boost her husband's already successful career, came through at precisely five o'clock the previous afternoon. The call, he insisted, was so important that she must, once again, forfeit her night out with the girls. But somehow the business call wasn't deemed important enough to interfere with his planned hunting trip with two fellow co-workers.

Her mission demanded she remain seated in his home office, near his personal phone line, until it rang, and then she was expected to write down the message, verbatim.

Kimberly, slightly embarrassed, but more fearful of her husband's wrath, had called her friends to cancel their weekly movie plans.

The weekly movie date, invented by her friends to allow her one night away from Bruce, doubled as the opportunity for them to confirm her well being. They had learned, several years earlier, not to question her last minute change of plans, or discuss her latest bruise.

They willingly joined her phony charade of a happy marriage to preserve what tiny fragment remained of her slowly fading dignity. Although they hid their observations well, she was certain they knew exactly how unhappy Bruce was making her life.

Attempting to assist her, or to encourage her to escape from his stranglehold, might possibly result in additional beatings for her. They anticipated that dreaded phone call informing them of the final attack, the fatal one that brought with it the sadness of knowing she would be gone from their lives forever.

Maintaining their friendship, with a watchful eye, was the best course of action they could offer.

Bruce, the current branch president of the Mountain High Bank in Denver, Colorado, planned to romance his way to the next level, chairman of the board—a mere steppingstone to the golden crown at the top, he told her.

Maximum focus and intense passion streamed into the execution of his flawless plan. Confident of his ownership of the new appointment, providing a vast increase in salary, the expected phone call was nothing more than an irritatingly, minor formality required to confirm his advancement.

Cornstalked

On the center of his desk, Bruce left Kimberly a neatly typed and printed, detailed set of instructions to handle the incoming call, including a well-thought-out script of responses to various comments the caller might convey.

The call was expected to arrive late afternoon, between four and five o'clock, on Friday, his second day of the male bonding weekend.

Bruce insisted Kimberly play the role of his private secretary, even though the call was being made to his home. She was instructed to inform the caller that Bruce was currently detained in a business meeting, and couldn't be interrupted, but he would be available to return the call within the hour. Immediately following the call, she was to contact him via his cell phone.

Kimberly skipped lunch on Friday. As a result, she found herself famished by early afternoon. She chose to eat her dinner earlier than their scheduled seven o'clock meal. Focused on the clock, rather than her meal, the flavor of the spaghetti and meat sauce went undetected as she swallowed each bite. At three forty-five, she placed her partially empty dishes into the sink, wiped her hands, and headed down the hall to Bruce's private office.

She paused outside the door, wiping her hands one last time on her old, faded, blue jeans—jeans she was not allowed to wear in his presence. She wanted to be certain there were no remnants of her dinner that might have been missed—a small speck of sauce that might go undetected until Bruce reached for the doorknob.

She slowly and cautiously entered his private domain. He had ordered her never to enter his office without permission. Paranoid and secretive, Bruce had hired a cleaning service to tend only to his office, and no other room of their spacious house. He hired the service to avoid any excuse that might give Kimberly the opportunity to snoop, under the guise of housekeeping.

To emphasize his demand for tightened security, he briefed her on the top-of-the-line security system he had installed to observe the housekeeper. Explaining the system to her in great detail was his twisted way of warning her that he could watch her every move, should she dare to enter the forbidden room.

With careful determination, her eyes scanned the room in search of the lens for the security camera, not wanting to block the view of the clock hanging on the wall. It was important to her that he sees precisely what time she entered, in the unfortunate event the caller neglected to follow through on schedule. She shuddered at the thought of his misdirected blame and the undeserved beating to follow.

She paced, checking her watch against the wall clock every few minutes. Attempting to regain her composure, she eased down gently into the burgundy leather, high-backed chair, with large-head brass tacks along the edge of the back and along the front of the armrests.

Sitting behind his desk, she ran her fingers over the intricately ornate carving along the desk's top edge. The bulk of their household furniture budget went into his office. She had to stretch out and make do with the remainder to furnish their entire home.

The rich cherry wood hue of the desk repeated throughout the luxurious room. Bruce had hired a woodcrafter to construct floor to ceiling bookcases from matching wood. The cabinets in the lower sections were always locked, but she'd never seen the keys. She preferred it that way; she couldn't be accused of searching the contents if she had no knowledge of the keys' location.

The top shelves contained Bruce's book collection. Image was everything with Bruce. He couldn't bear to have mismatched books lining the shelves. He had located a book restorer, with the help of an interior decorator who had come to him for a business loan. He chose to have the books re-covered with gold imprinted letters on either black or burgundy leather. At first glance, one would assume they were several volumes of complete sets.

An expensive hand-woven area rug covered the majority of the hardwood floor. No floral designs for Bruce, but rather a strongly masculine, geometric design flavored with dark forest greens, burgundy, and tans, accented in black.

After Kimberly glanced up at the clock, again, she removed his phone from the charger, pressed a button, and listened for the dial tone to be certain it was in proper working order. Then she quickly turned it off for fear the call might come through at that precise moment, causing the caller to inform Bruce that his personal line was busy when he attempted to contact him.

Kimberly wrung her hands and bit her lower lip. She bounced her knee up and down as she pressed her heel into the soft pile of the rug beneath the desk.

"Come on, come on, ring, will you," she said as she stared intently at the phone.

She lifted the script Bruce had prepared and read it again for the fiftieth time since he had left the house the previous morning. She could tell he was in a hurry to get on the road because he left before she had a chance to fix breakfast for him.

Her anxiety mounted as the time crept past. What if he wasn't going to call? What would she tell Bruce? What *could* she tell Bruce? How would he blame her this time? He'd find a way.

She watched the thin, burgundy, second hand on the clock ticking, as the large, black hand inched slowly to the top position. The sound of the phone ringing, even though she so anxiously awaited it, caused her to jump.

Cornstalked

She drew in a deep breath, sat straight up in the chair, threw back her shoulders, and prepared to answer on the second ring.

"Bruce Clarke's office," she said with a slight tremble in her voice.

"Is Mr. Clarke in?" asked the woman at the other end.

A woman? Bruce was expecting a call from a man, Mr. John Grimes to be exact. Why was his secretary calling? Then she quickly realized Mr. Grimes, a busy man, probably preferred to have his secretary handle the connection. After all, wasn't Bruce trying to portray his own image of importance by having her pretend to be his secretary, and inform Mr. Grimes he was too busy to be disturbed and couldn't take the call.

"I'm sorry, Mr. Clarke is in a meeting. May I take a message?" she responded. Her voice calmed in response to the less threatening female voice.

"There's no need for Mr. Clarke to return the call. Mr. Grimes wanted me to convey his sincere apologies to Mr. Clarke. He said to tell him it was a close race, but they will not be offering the job to Mr. Clarke. You will be sure to give him that message?" she asked.

Kimberly swallowed hard, "Yes. I will tell him."

She slumped back into the oversized chair, her heart raced as beads of perspiration formed on her forehead. Her vision faded as she felt the unmistakable queasy urge building deep within her stomach.

Jumping up from his chair, hoping to make it out of his office before losing her stomach contents, on his precious one-of-a-kind rug, she raced down the hall to the bathroom. With barely enough time to open the lid of the toilet, she experienced another round of projectile vomiting caused by the mounting stress.

She lost count of the times she'd vomited from her fear of Bruce's reaction to an incident she had little or no control over. In all the years they'd been married, she could only remember one episode where Bruce was ill enough to vomit.

He was aware of her weak stomach, as he put it— another sign of her anemic character. He prided himself in his ability to be in constant control over his emotions and not let anyone or anything cause him undue stress.

Her arms, folded over the rim of the toilet seat, offered support for her spinning head. The cold, clammy texture to her skin slowly subsided. She reached for a hand towel from the stack on the shelf nearby. After wiping her mouth, she ran the towel across the sweat on her forehead, loosening the strands of dark hair plastered to her skin. She rinsed her mouth then quickly brushed her teeth before calling Bruce.

"He's going to blame me," she whispered to herself. "Oh my god, what can I say?"

Cornstalked

Trembling, she made the call. His cell phone rang once...her breathing quickened. Twice...she bit her lip so hard it bled this time. Brushing her tongue across her lip, she removed the taste of blood.

Three rings...her breathing slowed, her pulse relaxed.

Could he be away from his phone? Would she be lucky enough to leave a message and not be subject to one of his ranting temper tantrums as he accused her of saying something that cost him his new position?

Four rings...it went to voicemail.

Where could he be? He knew the call would arrive no later than five, and it was now ten minutes past. What could he possibly be doing at that very moment that would prevent him from taking the call?

She waited patiently while his message played through. She cleared her throat and began, "Bruce, Mr. Grimes' secretary called. She said he wants you to accept his sincere apologies, but they've offered the position to someone else."

She set down his phone then raced back to the bathroom to throw cold water on her face and sip a cool glass of water. She studied her image in the mirror. Her dark brown eyes were sunken. Her face was prematurely aging from stress. She twisted her long, black hair into a roll and clipped it to the top of her head.

Bruce insisted she wear her hair down. Wearing it up when he wasn't home was her way of attempting to enjoy an ever-so-minor moment of control over some small portion of her unhappy life.

She straightened a few damp, stray hairs then sighed as she peered into the frightened eyes looking back at her. She knew it wasn't over; soon he'd listen to the voicemail. She prayed he'd have a few minutes to calm down before he returned her call—for whatever good praying did. How many times had she prayed for her own death while he was beating her? Or the times she asked God for a drunken driver to collide with Bruce in a fatal crash, eliminating him from her life.

She hoped he wouldn't call, but she knew he would. He called every night when he was away to be certain she was in. She waited. The hours passed slowly as she forced herself to stay awake. The entire night brought no word from Bruce. She waited until the sun was up before calling the sheriff's office.

CHAPTER 2

"Perkins County Sheriff's office," said Jason, the Saturday morning dispatcher. Jason, a single, thirty-something, had been working as the dispatcher for several years. Shortly after he took the position, he cut off his long, brown ponytail and removed his unruly attempt at a beard. Listening to other people's problems encouraged him to develop a new appreciation for his own life and lifestyle. Then, of course, there was the added incentive when he realized he looked more like the few prisoners they incarcerated each year than one of the good guys.

Today, he worked the seven-to-three shift.

"Hello," said Kimberly, her voice weak. "My name is Kimberly Clarke. Um...something may have happened to my husband."

Jason sat up straight in his chair, grabbed a pen, and prepared to take notes.

"What's your husband's name, and what do you think happened to him?"

"His name is Bruce, Bruce Clarke with an 'e'. He didn't call last night, and he always calls home," she started.

Jason smiled to himself. Must be newlyweds. Probably the first time hubby stayed out all night and didn't call home.

"I'll need some more information from you. Can I have your address and phone number, please?"

Kimberly grew more relaxed as she spoke. Jason's gentle voice soothed her frazzled nerves. The worst was over. She had actually made the call, and connected with a nice, young man who was willing to listen to her story without judgment. She quickly recited her address and phone number.

"You're from Denver?"

"Yes."

"Why are you calling our office?"

"I'm sorry, let me explain. My husband left here on Thursday morning to go pheasant hunting with his co-workers. He told me they'd be hunting around Grant. I went on the Internet and found your phone number. I haven't heard from him since Thursday night."

Cornstalked

"Is it possible his cell phone just died and he couldn't call you?"

"No, that's impossible. He has a car charger, and he's very conscientious about keeping it charged, in case I need to reach him."

"Are you sure he made it all the way out here?"

"Yes, he called Thursday night and told me about the drive. He said it snowed, but the roads were good, and he was expecting to get lots of birds."

"He's made contact within forty-eight hours, so technically, he's not really considered missing yet."

"I know, but you have to understand, he was expecting a very important phone call. He insisted I contact him as soon as it came in. And, he didn't answer his phone, and he hasn't called back," she said, knowing her concerns didn't sound like much of a reason to gather a search party, to go out in bad weather, for the sole purpose of finding her husband.

"What was the phone call about?"

At first, Kimberly felt the need to remain guarded about Bruce's personal business, but decided it might help the dispatcher understand the gravity of her situation.

"It was about a job promotion. He was pretty anxious to get that call."

"Did he get it?"

"The call?"

"No, the promotion?"

"Uh...no, he didn't."

"And, did you leave him a voicemail with the bad news?"

"Yes."

"Well, then maybe he didn't want to talk about it, so he didn't call you back. I'm sure he'll call later today. If you don't hear from him by tonight, give us a call back and we'll see what we can find out."

Confused and frightened, wondering why he hadn't contacted her, coupled with the thought of his anger regarding the disappointing news, she honestly hoped he wouldn't return her call.

She said, "Okay, I'll wait until tonight."

She tossed her cell phone down, beside her, onto the bed. Drawing her blanketed knees to her chest, she wrapped her arms tightly around them, and glanced at the clock. She had twelve hours to wait until she could officially call him missing, or thirty-six hours until he was due to return home.

Was it wrong to hope something had happened to him? Would that really make her such a terrible person? Her mind wandered as she looked around her bedroom. What would life be like without Bruce? Wonderful. That was an easy answer.

After rocking back and forth in an attempt to soothe her frayed nerves, she climbed out of bed to

Cornstalked

shower. She walked into their master bathroom to turn on the water when she realized she had left her phone on the bed. She raced back, picked it up from the bed, checked the charge, and pressed it to her chest, relieved that she hadn't forgotten it while she showered. The ring tone could have been muffled by the blankets, making it impossible to hear over the sound of the water spraying onto the glass shower door.

She knew if she missed Bruce's call, he would accuse her of missing Mr. Grimes' call, as well, then fabricating some story about him not getting the job. He might miss out on making the necessary return call, and the job would be given to someone much less deserving.

While the steaming water massaged her aching body, she gently slid the bar of soap slowly over her bruises that were still in various shades of healing—some reddish purple, others greenish yellow. Like most spouse abusers, he had learned to strike where no one would notice the discoloration.

It seemed he always managed to concoct a suitable reason to beat her when he planned to be away for a few days—a visible and painful reminder not to do anything that might upset him.

Without taking the time to towel dry, she pulled on her thick, white terrycloth bathrobe. She gathered the plush fabric close to her neck. She planned to wear it the

17

entire day—yet another way to enjoy her temporary freedom.

She stood before the mirror, combing through her long, black hair. Staying awake all night caused the dark circles beneath her eyes to deepen, and that, combined with the mascara that smeared during her shower, reminded her of the first time Bruce had struck out at her, blackening both of her eyes and breaking her nose.

Her mother and sister begged her to leave him, but instead, she stood up for him. She said he was a good man and they just didn't understand him. Bruce managed to sever the relationship she had with her family—another common control tactic practiced by abusers. He refused to allow her to attend her own mother's funeral. Her sister never forgave her for choosing Bruce over her own family. She was ostracized from the one security network she so desperately needed.

Happy to have the house to herself for the entire weekend, there was a slight bounce to her step. She could pretend she was no longer married to Bruce. She could pretend Bruce Clarke no longer existed. And she could even pretend he didn't return her phone call because her prayers had been answered, and he had met with an unfortunate accident.

She programmed the coffee maker to greet them in the morning with a hot pot of coffee—one less step for her to balance while fixing Bruce his daily breakfast of bacon and eggs, toast, hash browns, juice, and coffee. He insisted on a huge breakfast, even on the days she felt ill and had to drag herself out of bed.

As the aroma of freshly brewed coffee filled the kitchen, she removed an unopened carton of Rocky Road ice cream, which she had hidden in the back of the freezer. She slowly filled an oversized mug with the hot steaming coffee, and removed a spoon from the utensil tray in the drawer.

Placing the spoon and the mug on the table, she struggled to open the carton of ice cream. She not only planned to eat the Rocky Road for breakfast, but she also dared to eat it directly from the carton.

She enjoyed the way the hot coffee warmed her mouth, speeding up the rate the ice cream melted. As she slowly pulled the second spoonful into her mouth, playing with it on her tongue, savoring the sensation, the phone rudely interrupted her pleasure.

Startled, she swallowed quickly, as if Bruce would somehow be able to tell what she was doing. She wiped her lips then picked up her cell phone. It was then she realized the landline was ringing. She darted across their large kitchen to retrieve it before the ringing ceased.

"Hello," she said, not recognizing the number on the caller I.D.

"Hi, I hate to call so early in the morning. I'm Mary Jaeger, Drew's wife."

"Yes?" responded Kimberly while not having the slightest clue as to the identities of either Mary or Drew.

"Drew went hunting with Bruce, and I haven't heard from him. I was wondering if you've heard from Bruce? I called Gina, Rick's girlfriend, and she hasn't heard from Rick either."

"No, Bruce hasn't called. I knew he was going hunting with two co-workers, but I don't know their names. I'm sorry, I also didn't recognize your name," she said. "I talked to Bruce Thursday night and he said they arrived through the snowy roads without any difficulty."

"Thursday night?" asked Mary.

"Yes. He called about seven on Thursday night, and told me they made it safely."

"That impossible," said Mary. "They didn't leave until Friday morning. Bruce had already picked up Rick, and then they stopped by here to pick up Drew. They left here about six yesterday morning."

"I'm confused. Bruce left here at six on Thursday morning. If he didn't get to your house until yesterday morning, where was he?"

Mary quickly said, "I'm sorry to bother you, but if you hear from Bruce would you give me a call? I'll give you my number."

"No, that's okay, the caller ID has it," said Kimberly, barely focusing on her conversation with Mary.

Cornstalked

After she hung up the phone, she stood in front of the sink. As she looked out across their large, perfectly manicured lawn, she thought about Bruce. She had her suspicions that he might be having another affair, but wondering is one thing, and catching him in this lie is another—a lie she didn't dare mention.

CHAPTER 3

"Mighty quiet today," said Sheriff Morgan Danberg, as he hung his coat on a wooden peg, attached to the old wall in desperate need of a fresh coat of paint.

Quiet is the best way to describe nearly every morning in the small town of Grant, Nebraska. There's the occasional speeding ticket, a barking dog complaint, maybe a little shoplifting at the local drugstore, or bored teenagers vandalizing the back entrances to buildings or egging cars.

Sometimes on Saturday nights, there might be an altercation at one of the local bars and, of course, DUI's for both adults and teenagers. Drinking is the primary pastime, next to sports, for small towns whose populations barely top one thousand.

Cornstalked

Sheriff Danberg poured himself a cup of coffee, and sorted through the donuts left over from the previous morning. His large, strong hands snatched up a cake donut with chocolate icing. Once dipped into his hot coffee, the stale texture would all but disappear.

Before stepping into his office, he turned to the dispatcher and asked, "You get any calls this morning?"

"Just the usual. A couple lost hunting dogs, a few farmers complaining hunters are too close to their houses, and, oh yeah, some woman called from Denver about her missing husband."

"Her what?" smiled Danberg. His eyes, the same steely gray as the paint on the walls, sparkled.

"I know," Jason smiled back. "It appears he didn't call home last night, so she thinks he's missing."

"Did she give you any details?"

"I didn't ask. You know how it is, guys get together to go hunting, and they don't want to get heckled about having to call home and check in with the wife and kids. The main reason they go hunting in the first place is to get away, and prove their manhood."

"That's no lie. I'm actually surprised we haven't had to haul in some drunken hunters yet this season."

Danberg started to walk away then turned back and said, "Could you tell by the sound of her voice if there might be something to his disappearance?"

23

There was a kindness and concern to his voice that didn't match his large, burly frame. For a long time, he carried the nickname Matt Dillon from the old television show, *Gunsmoke*. It faded away as the younger generation of cops increased on the force. The title meant nothing to them.

"Hell, I couldn't tell. Why?" asked Jason.

"I don't know. Curious I guess. I'd hate to have some city idiots out there stranded in the cold all night long."

"I guess I hadn't thought of that. I suppose with the snow on the ground, they could've driven off into a drift somewhere, or ran out of gas, not realizing they might be twenty or more miles from the nearest town. I'll let you know if she calls back," said Jason, his curiosity equally aroused.

They've received calls on missing dogs, missing vehicles, and even missing teenagers, but a missing husband strayed from the norm.

Two hours later, Danberg stood from his desk. He stretched his arms high over his head and arched his back. He needed a break from the insanely boring paperwork. With his chin cupped in his hands, he turned his head, first to the right and then to the left, creating a series of tiny crackles and pops, as he relieved the stiffness from his neck.

Cornstalked

He carried his old, chipped, baby blue coffee mug back to the pot that had been warming for the past five hours. He filled his mug almost halfway then stopped when the unpleasant aroma of burned coffee met his nostrils.

"Any word from that woman about her husband?" he asked.

"Nope, nothing. It's really bothering you, isn't it?"

"I just keep picturing those sorry bastards wandering around with frostbite. How cold did it get last night?"

"Let me check. Last night's lows were supposed to be in the teens. It's only twenty-seven now, and it's nearly lunchtime. I suppose they could be a little cold if they *are* stranded."

"Why don't you give that woman a call and get a description of the vehicle for me. I'd feel better if I saw it parked at the café, and the guys were just too macho to call home."

Danberg inadvertently sipped the scorching hot coffee, but after the second swallow, when his taste buds confirmed what his nose had already told him, he poured the foul-tasting black fluid down the drain.

He returned to his desk covered with that morning's office work. Not able to force himself to continue, he gathered the scattered papers into tidy stacks, before putting on his hat and coat. The missing hunters offered a more palatable adventure.

Jason searched his desk for the note containing the contact information for Kimberly Clarke. The elusive scrap of paper had disappeared. He spun around in his chair to search the trash basket nearby, in case he had accidentally brushed it from his desk. His eye caught sight of the yellow sticky note attached to the tall, four-drawer, black file cabinet standing next to his desk. He must've stuck the note on the file cabinet without giving it serious consideration. He dialed the number Kimberly had given him earlier that morning.

"Hello," she said.

"Mrs. Clarke, this is Jason from the Perkins County Sheriff's Department. I'm calling to see if you've heard from..." he ran his finger across the slip of paper searching for the name. All the while telling himself his penmanship needed to improve, as well as his method of taking notes...he continued, "your husband, Bruce, this morning."

"No, not a word," she said. "Why are you calling? The forty-eight hours isn't up yet."

"I'm aware of that ma'am, but it's pretty quiet here this morning and the sheriff asked me to check with you. He just wants to be sure they didn't have to spend the night outside, stranded in their vehicle."

Cornstalked

"I'm sure they all have cell phones and would've called if they needed help," she pointed out.

"That's not always possible. We have dead areas where there's no phone reception. The locals know the spots, but traveling hunters would have no idea when they were approaching a dead spot, or where to walk to pick up a signal again."

"I didn't know about that," she said.

"In any event, can you give me a description of the vehicle and the names of the men with your husband? Oh, and the license number, too."

"Let's see, it's a 2010 Escalade. It's red, but I don't know the license number."

She felt guilty about *not* feeling guilty. Since the time Bruce failed to return her call, she'd been hoping something had happened to him. She tried to remain hopeful. What kind of woman wishes for the demise of her husband? Maybe one who has to nowhere else to turn?

"Can you tell me what Bruce was wearing?"

"No. He did his own packing," she said.

"How about his friends, what are their names?"

"I don't...wait a minute. Drew and um...um...Rick, yeah that's it. Drew and Rick."

"Do you have their last names?"

"I'm sorry, I don't. I've never met them. They work with my husband. But I could call Drew's wife and get those details for you."

"No, that's okay. I'm sure we won't need them. I'm sure they're probably fine. I'll call you back if we need more information."

"I suppose you get calls like this all the time from hunters' wives," she said, trying to make light of the situation.

"Actually, no. But, as I said before, I'm sure they're fine. I'll let you know if we spot them."

"Thank you," she said.

She hung up the phone and walked to the patio doors. Drawing open the draperies, she saw that snow had begun to fall and the lawn had disappeared beneath the thin, white blanket. Opening the door, she stepped out onto the doormat, sheltered by the overhanging floor from the decking above.

Bruce had chaise lounges set on the deck outside their bedroom's French doors. He forced her to strip and sit outside with him. It didn't matter to him if it was day or night. He wanted to enjoy her body in various lights. However, he often preferred moonlight, when her bruises were exceptionally large. Then he insisted she have sex with him outdoors, knowing the neighbors could watch if they tried hard enough to see through the branches of the trees separating the yards.

Wrapping her thick robe tightly around her tiny body, she watched as the snowflakes change from small, insignificant, flat, ovals to the large, feathery, flakes that

Cornstalked

floated every so gently to the ground, disappearing as they clung to the millions already joined together forming the blanket.

She spotted a robin that had failed to migrate and was trapped in Denver for a long, cold, Colorado winter. Attempting to fight off the bone-chilling cold, he had puffed up his the gray underfeathers, paling the rust coloring on his breast. His small, black eyes were closed as he huddled on the ground beneath a bush.

"Poor little bird," whispered Kimberly. "You look so cold."

Kimberly loved animals, not just birds, and cats, and dogs, but all animals. She desperately wanted a pet. Any pet would do. But Bruce refused to allow an animal into their home.

When he said they'd shed, she suggested a poodle or a schnauzer. When he said he didn't want them crapping and peeing all over the carpets, she suggested a bird. When he said he was allergic to feathers, she mentioned a hamster. Of course, he didn't want some disease-ridden rodent causing them to develop some fatal disease.

Since he didn't like rodents, she brought up the idea of a pet snake. It wouldn't shed—fur at least—and it wouldn't make a mess in the house, and it would eat mice.

That was a mistake. He slapped her across the room and accused her of wanting a snake so she could moonlight as a stripper. How he made that connection was beyond her, but then, he had a real talent for twisting her words to make up some totally preposterous storyline.

He finally agreed to allow her to have one goldfish, in a bowl in the laundry room, where she couldn't even sit and enjoy it. Although she couldn't pet it or cuddle with it, at least it was hers, and she looked forward to visiting the tiny fish twice a day when she went in to feed it.

Her thoughts turned back to Bruce. If he was stranded in his vehicle overnight, she wondered how cold he was at that very moment. Maybe he wasn't even in the vehicle. Maybe he had no shelter from the weather at all.

She closed her eyes and imagined him lying on the ground in a ditch alongside the road. Maybe he'd been hit by oncoming traffic while searching for a ride to town for fuel. Or, maybe he had driven his precious Escalade into a tree.

She squeezed her eyes tightly, wanting to hold on to the deadly image she conjured in her hopeful mind. The gruesome scene faded. Quickly it was replaced with him, not cold or abandoned, but warm and comfortable while making love to his mistress. Did she have bruises covering her body, too? Or did he reserve his morbid artwork for his wife alone?

CHAPTER 4

Danberg tore Jason's notes from his desk pad. He planned to drive through town and look for the missing hunters.

This time Jason had penned the words in a more legible hand.

"Not much to go on," said the sheriff as he read the notes. "But I'll cruise town and check for a 2010 Red Escalade with Colorado plates. Call me if you find out anything else."

The interior air of the sheriff's car mirrored the outside temperature, minus the wind. While the car's engine warmed, Danberg rubbed his aching hands together. He pressed his mouth to his cupped hands and blew into them, hoping to warm his cold fingers. His frosty breath spread out from his hands and rose to the ceiling of the car, where it disappeared into the cloth covering. After a brief and futile attempt to warm his hands, he dug deep into his coat pockets until he found his gloves. With his fingers already growing stiff, he struggled to pull the gloves onto hands that seemed one size too large for the gloves.

The parking lot's surface was rough with ice that crunched beneath the tires when he backed his car out of the *Reserved for Sheriff* parking spot, to turn around before pulling out onto the main street.

The sheriff's department shared space with the courthouse, a common practice in small towns. Since it was Saturday, all other offices in the Perkins County Courthouse were closed. Jason's car and the sheriff's car, along with two four-wheel drive pickups owned by the sheriff's department, were the only vehicles taking up a very small portion, at the west end, of the otherwise empty lot.

Danberg hesitated at the stop sign along the edge of the main drag. His eyes surveyed the street, hoping to spot the red vehicle quickly—no luck.

The narrow, angled parking spots lining the street in front of the tiny, privately owned stores remained nearly empty on Saturdays during inclement weather.

The locals learned the wise lesson a long time ago, passed from generation to generation, to stock up with extra supplies during the winter. That included groceries, animal feed, bottled water, and to purchase toilet paper in the largest packages available. In the event of a severe storm—winds always accompanied both rain and snow in Perkins County—the roads could become impassible for several days.

If ice accumulated on the power lines or if lightning struck a transformer, repairs to the electrical lines might take anywhere from a few minutes, to a week, and sometimes longer.

Most farmers use alternative sources of heat, such as a fireplace, a wood burning stove, or a generator, especially if they have livestock requiring fresh water. The weather in rural areas has been known to show no mercy during storms.

Danberg slowly cruised the three-block business district. His eyes scanned the parking areas for a red SUV. He spotted a few Escapes and Blazers but no Escalades. He looked down the side streets to be certain they hadn't parked around a corner and walked to the drugstore or café, though that was highly unlikely with the abundance of available parking.

He pulled over along the curb, near the Hastings Memorial Library, where he had a clear view of the two small convenience stores. They both handled high volumes of foot traffic from seasonal strangers in a hurry to grab a quick snack, or pick up supplies they neglected to pack, or simply to replenish their weekend cache of beer.

Sadly, there were no signs of them at either store. His final fleeting hope was to find them at the southernmost end of town, parked in the grocer's lot.

He paused to wait for a gap in traffic, that is, if you can call two or three cars traffic, then he turned south toward Hatch's, the only grocery store in town. Although there were more vehicles in that lot than anywhere else in town, the Escalade was not among them.

He circled the three-row parking lot then parked at the west edge, where he could watch traffic coming and going, hoping to spot the three hunters presumed missing.

Several black Labrador retrievers stood in the beds of pickup trucks and barked back and forth at each other. Generally, when a farmer brings his dog to town, it remains in the back of the pickup, no matter how tempting a situation might develop providing them with more fun than standing and waiting.

But when the once-a-year hunters arrived in the county with their family pets, purchased to become prized hunting dogs, those dogs lacked the obedience training required to resist temptations—thus a phone call to the sheriff's department reporting their dog stolen or lost.

An elderly couple parked next to him. He watched as they cautiously stepped from their old, blue Buick. A

Cornstalked

frail, little, man trying to help a frail, little, woman maintain her footing on the ice.

Danberg pushed his hat down hard on his head and stepped out.

"Here, let me help you," he said, offering his arm to the wife.

"Oh, dear," she giggled. "Be careful, he might get jealous. There's no telling how bad he'll hurt you."

Her husband looked over at the tall, strong, sheriff and said, "You touched her; she belongs to you now."

"Oh you," she laughed.

Danberg never tired of the sweet, old folks in his town. He carefully guided the wife to the store's entrance, all the while walking close enough to the husband to swoop him up if he should lose his balance on the ice. All three knew what he was doing, and it was sincerely appreciated.

After he deposited the kind couple at the door, he stumbled and slid his way back to his own car. How embarrassed he would've been if *he* had been the one to lose his balance while helping them, and had taken them both down with him.

He paused before entering his vehicle. He returned to the store.

Cheryl smiled when he walked in the door, "Good morning, Morgan."

"Morning Cheryl, is Barb in?"

35

"Upstairs."

As he walked through the store, he stopped
Valerie. You haven't noticed three strange men in here
today or yesterday have you?"

"This is hunting season, so there are lots of
strangers in and out of here."

"Thanks," he said as he finished his walk through
the store to the back where he climbed the stairs to Barb's
office.

He tapped on the door as he entered.

"Morning," she said. "What can I do for you?"

"I'm looking for three men in a red Escalade from
Colorado. Can you tell all of your employees to keep an
eye out for them for me?"

"Sure, did they do something wrong?"

"No, they're missing and their wives are looking for
them."

"We'll give you a call if we see them," she said.

"Thanks," he said as he turned and walked away.

As he passed Kevin and Ben in the produce
department, he tipped his hat.

Barb called down to the front register and when
Marnee answered she said, "Tell Patti, and Crystal and
anyone else who's working today to watch for three
hunters in a red Escalade and call me or the sheriff's
department if you see them."

"Anything wrong?" asked Marnee.

Cornstalked

"No, their wives are looking for them."

Danberg left the store and once again slid back to his car. Just as he was about to climb into his car, he spotted a red Escalade turning north from a side street, at the opposite end of town from where he had parked. Excited, he hurried into his car.

He eased forward and waited for two semis hauling corn to pass before he pulled out onto the street. With his eyes fixed on the red SUV, he followed the semis until they were just north of town then he passed at the first opportunity.

By then, the SUV was nearly two miles ahead of him, but still in clear view on the straight, flat highway. Pressing hard on his accelerator, he narrowed the gap. As the distance between the sheriff and the Escalade continued to decrease, he confirmed the Escalade had Colorado license plates. Danberg turned on his lights and siren, signaling the driver to pull over.

The driver caught sight of him in his rearview mirror and eased his way to the shoulder, but not before glancing at his speedometer, ready to defend an accusation of speeding. The three passengers—two men and a woman—watched as the sheriff approached.

The driver rolled down his window, with his wallet in hand, he apparently knew the drill.

"Was I speeding?"

"No. I'm looking for Bruce Clarke. Is that you?"

"No, sir."

Danberg glanced inside at the other man who shook his head no.

"You haven't seen another red Escalade with Colorado plates out and about, have you?" he asked.

"Not since yesterday morning," said the driver. "You always notice when someone's driving the same vehicle."

"You say you did see one yesterday morning?"

"Yeah, about nine or so."

"Where?"

"Out in the country about fifteen miles west of here," said the driver. "Did he do something wrong?"

"No, I have a message from a wife for one of the passengers. Can you tell me how many people were in it?"

The driver stared out over the hood of his vehicle while he tried to recall the brief encounter with the other Escalade.

The man in the passenger seat said, "Three. There were three men. I noticed them, too, because of what they were driving."

"Okay, thanks. Drive safe and stay warm," said Danberg. He tapped the side as they drove away.

Once inside his car, he contemplated turning back to the south, where the main street intersects with Highway Twenty-Three, and then driving west, but if they had been seen there over twenty-four hours earlier, he knew it would, most likely, be a waste of his time.

Which direction offered him the greatest chance of locating them? He turned to look back toward the south. His stomach interrupted his thoughts when it objected to having had nothing in it that morning, other than a stale donut and bad coffee.

Driving further out of town on an empty stomach meant he'd be really hungry by the time he returned over an hour later. Then if, perhaps, he ran across the hunters needing help changing a flat tire or jump-starting their engine, he could be delayed even longer.

The most logical plan would be to grab a bite to eat before heading out to search. That way he could stay out until dusk, if he felt the need.

He backed his car onto the shoulder of the road, then turned around and drove back into town to the café.

The small town café was always filled to capacity with pheasant hunters the first week the season opened, especially after a good snow. Snow in the forecast means improved conditions for diehard hunters who are properly dressed.

Cold pheasants will hunker down in the brush, trying to conserve heat and energy to stay warm. When the birds are aware of a hunter's approach and fear being discovered, they'll wait until the very last moment, when they are only two or three feet away from the hunter, then take flight. The sound of a nide of pheasants suddenly taking to the air, without notice, will, without fail, startle anyone who happens to be that close.

Inside the café, a small line formed near the front door, waiting for a table to clear. Danberg fell into line behind the last man. He listened to the chatter about the birds who got away, much like a fisherman's tale.

He glanced around the room. Nearly every table had men, and a few tables had women who accompanied the men. They were donned in hunting garb, speaking rapidly and loudly.

The young waitresses were darting back and forth from the kitchen to the tables, attempting to provide good service to everyone. It was obvious they weren't accustomed to large crowds by the way they appeared to be totally overwhelmed.

"Hey, Morgan. Over here," called a voice from the center of the room.

His eyes scanned over the heads of the customers dressed in camouflaged jackets with matching pants. Most of them kept their hats on, planning to eat and run. Besides, at most tables, there were no wives to scold them for their lack of manners—wearing their hats indoors.

Danberg recognized his neighbor, Jack, his arm waving and pointing to an unoccupied chair at his table.

Danberg stepped out from his last place in line and eased his way through the group waiting at the cash

Cornstalked

register. He smiled and waved to the familiar townspeople he saw along his way. He searched the faces of strangers devouring cheeseburgers, fries, and bowls of chili. He wanted to remember the faces in case one of the tables contained the missing hunters, so that if later in the day, Kimberly scanned a photo into her computer to send to them, he would recognize the men.

Finally, he made his way to Jack's table.

"Busy day, huh?" asked Jack, as he took a bite from his cheeseburger oozing with catsup and mustard that fell back onto his plate in quiet plops, landing on his French fries.

The frazzled waitress quickly approached, "The usual, Sheriff?"

"Sure."

She disappeared into the kitchen to place his order and returned with a hot pot of coffee. She smiled as she carefully turned his white, porcelain cup right side up then filled it to the brim with the steaming hot liquid.

Everyone knew Danberg was single, and that the unmarried women of the town kept an eye open for good men who might be husband material.

He smiled back and watched the crimson color rise from just above her breasts, up her neck, until the color finally reached her face, flushing all the way to her forehead.

Danberg picked up the cup and blew over the top of the coffee before sampling. He knew, with such a large crowd, the coffee machines were busy and the coffee was freshly brewed, not stale and burnt like his previous cup.

He savored the robust flavor, and enjoyed the way the coffee moved down his throat, warming his chilled body.

"So, anything new and exciting going on in town that we should know about?" asked Jack.

"Nope, same ol', same ol'," said Danberg.

"Do you ever miss working in the city?"

"Nope, this is almost like being retired," he smiled, as he shook a packet of sugar into his coffee to take the bite out.

Jack noticed the sheriff's eyes frequently glancing out through the storefront window.

"Looking for somebody?" asked Jack.

"Maybe," said Danberg. "I have a message for a hunter from his wife. I'm just watching for a red Escalade to pass through town."

"I saw one heading north about ten minutes ago," said Jack.

"Not the right one. I already checked it out."

The waitress returned to the table with a bowl of steaming chili, thick with beans and meat. She had added a spoonful of sour cream to the top, just the way Danberg liked it.

Cornstalked

He moved his coffee cup to make room for the cheeseburger and fries, homemade—peel left on and deep fat fried—the cheeseburger hand pressed and grilled to perfection. Lastly, she set down a slice of pumpkin pie topped with a large dollop of whipped cream that oozed down the side, pooling onto the plate.

Danberg touched the whipped cream with his spoon to center it.

The two men continued their casual, meaningless conversation, never again making eye contact, as they both watched intently, through the window, for the mysterious red SUV.

Each time the door opened, and a new group of hunters entered, Danberg switched his stare from the window to the faces of the men, then back to the window.

The Sheriff finished his cheeseburger, chili, and fries in record time.

The waitress returned to remove his empty plates. She walked away, sad that he ignored her presence while he continued to stare out of the window.

He turned his attention back to the table and his piece of pumpkin pie. He cut a large chunk from the pointed tip, smeared it around in the whipped cream, and then slid it into his mouth. How he loved pumpkin pie. Might even be his favorite. Normally, he would have taken his time to enjoy each bite, but that day he quickly gobbled it up.

Danberg wiped the whipped cream from his lips, drained the last bit of coffee from his cup then left the table to head to the men's room.

When he returned, Jack had already left. Danberg added to the tip Jack had left on the table then walked to the front of the café where he stood in line to sign his tab. No need to pay with cash or credit card. All he had to do was sign his name to be billed at the end of the month.

Larry, a local farmer, walked up to stand in line behind Danberg.

"Hear you're looking for some guys in a red Escalade."

Word travels fast in a small town, and after Danberg's first year as sheriff, the speed in which it traveled no longer surprised him.

"That's right. Colorado plates. Let me know if you see it."

CHAPTER 5

Angry with Rick for not calling, Gina listened while the phone rang three times before she answered. She didn't want to give him the impression she was waiting by the phone for his call. Her feelings were hurt. Why didn't he have the courtesy to call earlier? Obviously, he had no qualms about breaking his promise to call her twice a day. She planned to be extremely cold and uncaring when she spoke to him, unless, of course, he had a good explanation and was overly apologetic.

Gina had tried to persuade Rick not to go hunting. Actually, he didn't want to go, but he felt he couldn't turn down Bruce's invitation. His promotion was on the line, and he realized it would be a bad move on his part to miss the opportunity to buddy up to Bruce, especially if it meant a nice pay increase was in his future by spending the entire weekend with his boss.

"Hello," she said coolly.

"Gina, this is Mary. Have you heard from Rick yet?"

"No, I thought you were Rick. He promised he'd call every morning and every night, but nothing since he left. Why? Haven't you heard from Drew either?"

"No, and I called Bruce's wife, Kimberly, and she hasn't heard from Bruce either," said Mary.

"Oh, so they all agreed together not to call us. I, for one, am not going to sit around this house and wait for Rick's call," said Gina.

"I know from what Drew says, that Bruce can be a little overbearing, but I also know Drew would sneak away to call me, even if he had to text from a stall in the men's room. I'm getting a little worried."

"Should we call Kimberly back to see if she's heard from Bruce?"

"I don't think that's a good idea. I already let it slip when I talked to her earlier that Bruce didn't pick Drew up until yesterday morning."

"What do you mean? Let what slip?" asked Gina.

"Drew says Bruce is a player. He's been having an affair with some woman who came in for a loan. Her credit was bad, but he signed her up anyway, you know, a leg loan."

Cornstalked

"Yeah, Rick told me the same thing. Bruce is a sucker for a pretty woman with bad credit. He gets a lot of action on the side that way," said Gina.

"Anyway, Kimberly thought Bruce left for the hunting trip on Thursday morning. My hunch is he was with another woman until he picked up Rick and Drew yesterday."

"You're right. Let's not call her. I don't want to have to answer questions about her husband. Anyway, I doubt if she'd appreciate the truth," said Gina.

"What should we do? Drew's not answering my messages, not even my texts," said Mary.

"Do you think there's a chance they never made it?" asked Gina. "Could they have had a car accident along the way?"

"That's what I'm afraid of," said Mary. "We haven't heard from any of them since they left, and the roads could've been bad."

"I checked yesterday's weather for the area they were supposed to be hunting in," stated Gina. "Cold and sunny in the morning, turning colder, with wind and cloud cover by the afternoon. I wrote it down in case he wanted me to check the forecast for him."

Gina picked up her favorite photo of Rick, dressed in a tux, from their last Valentine's Day dinner. He had rented a limousine and a tuxedo with tails then met her at the door with flowers and chocolates.

She ran her finger lovingly across his face, stopping at his lips that she outlined with the tip of her perfectly manicured plum-colored nail.

Mary broke the moment of silence.

"Gina, are you still there? Are you okay?"

"Now, I'm starting to worry," said Gina. "I was so mad at Rick and didn't want to talk to him, but now I'd give anything to hear his voice."

"I don't know where they're staying. Do you?" asked Mary.

"I do. I wrote that down, too. Let's see." She paused to read through her notes. "They were planning to stay at the Sunsetter's Motel. I even have the phone number."

"Are you always so efficient?"

Gina smiled proudly to herself before she answered, "Yeah, it's a curse sometimes. I'll call the motel and see if they checked in. I'll call you right back."

Gina dialed the number.

"Sunsetter's Motel."

"I'd like to leave a message for my boyfriend, Rick Mulligan. He checked in yesterday with two other hunters."

"Hold on. We're full to capacity and they're all hunters."

Gina waited.

Cornstalked

"Yes, he's sharing a room with Drew Jaeger. They were with their boss, at least he told me he was their boss. The boss guy asked for a double room to himself. I suppose he's expecting his wife to join him later today."

"Great, so they did check in then," said Gina, relieved.

"I can ring his room for you if you'd like."

"Yes, please."

Gina waited.

The woman's voice came over the phone. "There's no answer."

"I don't suppose you know what time they left this morning?" asked Gina.

"Oh, they didn't sleep here last night. When I went to clean their rooms this morning all of their luggage was still sitting on the beds, but the beds hadn't been slept in. I know that because I have some customers who like to make their own beds, but I fold one corner of the top sheet, at the head of the bed, different, so I can tell if the bed's been slept in. That way I know if I need to change the sheets. All three beds were untouched."

"Are you sure?" asked Gina. "Are you absolutely sure?"

"Yes, ma'am."

"Okay, thanks."

"Wait, don't you want to leave a message?"

"Yeah, if any of them show up tell them to call home."

Gina paced around the apartment. She clicked her fingernails together while she walked. *Click, click, click.* She was oblivious to the sound of her habit, but it irritated the hell out of Rick.

She couldn't quite put the story together in her mind. Where are they? Where could they have gone? Why didn't Rick call? Why didn't any of them call? What would she tell Mary? And, what about Kimberly? Should she call her? A tear fell silently down her cheek as she stopped in front of Rick's photo.

"Where are you?" she asked his image trapped behind the glass.

She focused on the phone then tightly pressed her eyes closed as she attempted to send her thoughts out into space, willing Rick to call—but nothing. The phone didn't ring.

She knew Mary would be anxiously awaiting her call. Stalling was not an option. Slowly, she dialed the number, still uncertain as to how to share with her the vague bits of information given to her by the woman from the motel.

Mary picked up the phone on the first ring, "Well?"

"I spoke to the lady who runs the motel. She said they made it in yesterday. They checked in at the office and she gave them their keys. She confirmed they had dropped off their luggage. Rick and Drew are sharing a room. Bruce had a double to himself, waiting for his wife to join him," Gina spewed out the words quickly, and as if they were rehearsed.

"Yeah, right, his wife. So, what time did they leave this morning?"

Gina sighed then paused to choose her words carefully.

Before she had the opportunity to compose a sentence, Mary jumped in. "What's wrong? I heard that sigh."

"They checked in, but they didn't sleep there last night."

"What!"

"That's what the woman said. She explained how she has a special way of making the bed to check to see if the sheets need to be changed, and they hadn't slept there."

"She what? Special way to make the bed? I don't get it," said Mary.

"I know, I know. She said she folds back a top corner so she won't have to make the bed if it wasn't slept in. Small towns, you know."

"Oh my god. Do you think something really did happen to them?" asked Mary.

Gina responded, "I'll have to admit, I'm more than just a little worried."

"What should we do?" asked Mary.

"I think it's time to call the police and report them missing. They might've had a hunting accident or a stalled car. They might be stranded somewhere."

"Are there any wild animals out there?" asked Mary.

"I don't think so. I guess maybe coyotes, but I don't think there's bears or anything. I really don't know," said Gina, not wanting to think about Rick and wild animals.

"Coyotes are bad enough after all the attacks that have been happening here in the Denver area. If they were out walking, without the SUV, they might not have been able to outrun a whole pack of them."

"Wait a minute. All three of them have guns. I doubt they were attacked by a pack of coyotes, or anything else," said Gina. "I'll call the police department."

"How will you get the number?" asked Mary.

"I just Googled it. I'll talk to you later."

Gina dialed the number.

"Perkins County Sheriff's Department."

"Hello, my name is Gina Barclay. My boyfriend and two other men are hunting in your area and they seem to be missing."

"What do you mean missing?" asked Jason. The caller piqued his curiosity after Kimberly's phone call earlier that morning.

Cornstalked

"They were supposed to call home, all three of them, and not one of them has."

"Were they driving a red Escalade, by chance?"

Gina's heart sank to her stomach. Her palms began to perspire. Her breathing quickened.

Her voice trembled when she answered, "Yes. Why? Were they in some sort of an accident?"

"No, ma'am. I didn't mean to frighten you. It's just we received a call this morning from the wife of one of your boyfriend's companions. Do you have any proof that they made it this far?"

"Yes, they checked into a motel there, but they didn't sleep there last night."

"Which motel?"

"The Sunsetter."

Jason took down all the necessary information then called Sheriff Danberg on his cell phone.

"What's up?" asked Danberg.

"You know the guy missing in the red Escalade?" started Jason.

"Yeah, I stopped the wrong one earlier today," said Danberg. "They told me they'd seen another one yesterday morning. Why? Is there something new?"

"Yep. Seems there were three guys in it and all three were supposed to call home, and all three haven't been heard from since they left."

"Damn hunters. They probably stopped somewhere else along the way, and didn't even make it all the way here. You know how those idiots can be at times. See a few birds along the way, and set up camp in a completely different town."

"Not this time," said Jason. "They set up camp over at the Sunsetter. Problem is, they never returned to camp. Their beds hadn't been slept in and their luggage is still there."

Danberg looked up toward the sky, clouds had moved in, and snow had begun to fall.

"Poor stupid bastards," he mumbled.

CHAPTER 6

Not having much luck locating the missing hunters, and with the weather taking a possible turn for the worse, Danberg abandoned his search and drove back to town.

Once he returned to his office, Sheriff Danberg contacted the neighboring towns of Imperial, Madrid, Ogallala, and Holyoke to ask their sheriff's departments to keep an eye out for all 2010 red Escalades.

His announcement to the other departments was brief but to the point.

"We have three hunters from the Denver area who have been reported missing. Their arrival to Perkins County has been confirmed. They checked into a local motel, but have not been seen or heard from since. I would appreciate any assistance you can give us."

After sending out the APB for the missing men, he started out the door.

"What are you going to do?" asked Jason.

"I'm going to get into the four-wheel drive, and go looking for them. If they're not stranded or hurt, they're gonna wish they had been when I get my hands on them."

Jason knew the sheriff well enough to know his concerns ran deep. He rarely lost his temper or made unnecessary threats like the one he'd just made.

"What do you want me to do?" asked Jason.

"Call in a couple guys to help comb the country roads. If they *are* stranded, and as cold as it is, I'm not sure what we're gonna find."

Jason prepared to make the calls.

Danberg returned through the office door, and walked over to Jason's desk. Jason set the phone down to give him his undivided attention.

"Keep me posted," said Danberg. "I don't want us wasting time and gas by covering the same roads. It's going to be your job to direct the search from your desk."

"Where are you starting?"

"I'll head west on Highway 23 until I hit the Phillips County line. You might call Holyoke and tell them to start right away. We'll meet at the county line.

Cornstalked

"After that, I'll head north one mile, and then drive back toward the east. Call those women back and find out if they hunt with anyone local, you know, a friend or family member."

Danberg could only hope they'd given up hunting for pheasants and they were off at some friends' home drinking and playing pool, or watching sports on cable television, all cozy and warm.

But somehow his instincts as a cop told him otherwise.

Jason placed the call to Holyoke first then dialed Kimberly. He saved contacting their deputies until he had finished speaking to Bruce's wife.

"Mrs. Clarke. This is Jason from the Perkins County Sheriff's Department. I need more information."

"You didn't find them?"

"No, not yet."

She paused, while she contemplated sharing her thoughts with the unknown dispatcher who had such a kind voice. Then she came to the conclusion that Bruce, and his infidelity, might be causing hardworking, innocent men into go out in bad weather to track him down unnecessarily.

She decided to tell Jason about Bruce's unfaithfulness.

"I think it's possible that they're not even there. I think my husband is having an affair, and he may have used this hunting trip as an excuse to stay with another woman."

That blew Jason's newlywed theory all to hell. He took a moment to digest the information she shared then continued with his search for more details.

"I know they made it this far, Mrs. Clarke..."

"Please, call me Kimberly," she said. She hated the sound of Mrs. Clarke. Being called by her married name intensified the controlled feeling, and the sound of her title somehow seemed like Bruce legitimately owned her just because she married him.

Jason continued, "They did check into the motel, and their luggage is still there. The sheriff wants to start searching for them before the snow gets any heavier."

"What information do you want from me?" she asked.

"Can you give us the names of any friends or family that they might be staying with, or visiting, while they're here?"

"No, sorry. I don't even know the last names of the men Bruce was with. I can call and get that."

"No, that won't be necessary. I spoke to the girlfriend of one of the men." He checked his notes for names. "She said Rick hasn't called home yet. She told me that Drew's wife hasn't heard from her husband either."

"Do you still think they're fine?" asked Kimberly.

Cornstalked

Guilt finally surfaced. She may have wished for the demise of her own husband, but she certainly wished no harm to come to his companions.

"Ma'am, it's too soon to say. Someone will call you when we find them."

"You sound confident that you'll find them," said Kimberly

"Yes, ma'am, absolutely. If they're still in the county, we *will* find them. I can promise you that. Try not to worry," said Jason, attempting to ease her anxiety.

Worry? She was still hoping for bad news. She wanted Jason to call her with the news that they found Bruce's body. No, how about they found his mangled body—indicating he had died a long, slow, painful death. She shook the thought from her mind; disappointed with the way Bruce made her think. That's not the kind of person she wanted to be.

Jason called Gina next to ask her for the same contact information for a local family or friend. The response was the same. Gina had no new names to share. Finally, he spoke with Mary and, unfortunately, she couldn't offer additional information either. The lack of clues lead the sheriff's department to a dead end.

He walked to the window when he noticed that the size of the snowflakes had doubled since the sheriff had left. He called in the re-enforcements.

When the extra deputies, Charlie and Fred, arrived, Jason said, "Okay, here's the scoop, guys. We have three hunters presumed missing. They arrived in Perkins County yesterday morning and checked into the Sunsetter Motel.

"Rick Mulligan, Bruce Clarke, and Drew Jaeger have not been seen since they checked into the Sunsetter around 10 a. m. yesterday morning. They were last seen leaving the parking lot, heading south on Central Avenue. They're driving a 2010 red Escalade with Colorado plates.

"Sheriff Danberg has contacted law enforcement in the surrounding towns to help with the search and rescue in their counties. He's headed west on Highway 23 to the state line."

Jason pointed to Danberg's route on the map.

"Once he leaves the state line, he's going north one mile then turning back to the east until he reaches town. He left me in charge of plotting your courses.

"I want one of you to drive north to the county line then head west until you reach the Phillips County line then turn south one mile and drive back toward town.

"I'll handle that route," said Charlie.

Charlie didn't appreciate going out into the cold to search for three men who probably made some bad judgment calls. After ten years as a deputy, he had to admit this was the first time he had to search for missing hunters. In all those years, if all the hunters he came across had the good sense to be aware of their surroundings and take the necessary precautions to stay safe then he assumed the mental capacities of the three they were going to be searching for were lacking common sense, or, possibly dampened by an overindulgence of alcohol. Regardless, their actions caused him to forfeit his day off. He had planned to watch the Nebraska football game from the comfort of his living room chair.

"Then I want you, Fred, to start in the middle…" they looked at the map, "halfway between Highway 23 and the north county line. Drive west until you hit the county line then go north one mile and head back east to town.

"Once you're in town, move over one mile and drive west again. We need to scour every east and west road before the sun sets."

Fred held a completely opposite attitude toward the situation than Charlie. He was bored with the lack of excitement he experienced in his first year as a cop. This was to be his first search and rescue assignment. He finally felt he had an important task to handle.

Once they decided Charlie would go to the northern edge and Fred would start in the middle, they plotted their courses on the map. Jason informed Danberg that Charlie and Fred were briefed about the situation and they were ready to begin.

After Danberg had confirmed the plan, and the deputies left the office, Jason called in an order for a sandwich from the café. He asked if, under the circumstances, someone could deliver it the office. He knew the café doesn't offer delivery. He begged and pleaded until they felt sorry for him and agreed to have one of the waitresses go out into the nasty, cold weather to make sure he didn't go hungry. But he owed them and they wouldn't forget his debt to them.

Jason knew he wouldn't be going home any time soon, even though his shift was ready to end. Carol had the shift following his, starting at three o'clock, but he couldn't walk out on his duties, especially since he was handling the three officers' routes from his desk. He poured another cup of coffee and waited for radio or cell phone contact from the crews.

Sheriff Danberg drove slowly along Highway 23, checking each side road and the ditches along the way, for any sign of a red vehicle. The two-lane highway had rough ice from a full week of evening storms. The midday thawing throughout the week turned the snow and ice into brown slush that froze solid again during the night.

The road crew had had a difficult time trying to keep up, but their attempts were futile. What the road crew hoped for was two days in a row of strong sunlight, without the afternoon clouds, to help the potentially treacherous road situation return to normal winter driving conditions.

Cornstalked

Along the sides of the roads were either large cedar tree windbreaks blocking Danberg's view across the land, or summer harvested wheat fields whose stubble caught the snow, leaving their adjacent patches of the highway less icy than others.

Then there were the cornfields in various stages of harvest. The snowy weather had moved in, prohibiting most farmers from finishing the harvest or, for some, their harvest had not yet begun.

Actually, this year's harvest of popcorn was the only corn harvest completed. Most of the fields of feed corn were still too wet for an early harvest, compounded by the snowfall, meaning some farmers might still be harvesting their corn at Christmas time, if not later.

Danberg strained to look deep into the rows of corn. The dryland corn had a considerably thinner stand, allowing limited visibility down the rows. While the irrigated corn made it impossible to see beyond the first five feet.

He rubbed the palm of his left hand across the barely-there whisker stubble on his left cheek—a nervous habit he had developed when something didn't feel quite right. This was one of those times. His instincts as a cop made him uneasy about the search.

Something told him those men were in trouble, serious trouble, and he didn't mean from the women in their lives. Attempting to survive a night in freezing cold weather, when you're not an experienced outdoorsman, could prove to be fatal.

"Poor, damn stupid, bastards," he repeated. "May God help you."

Danberg had once worked for the police department in Los Angeles, California. The criminal climate had drastically changed over the years, and not in a good way. Shooting a cop didn't seem to have the same affect on criminals. The newer generation lacked respect for everyone and everything, including uniformed police officers.

Danberg's wife had constantly begged him to quit. She suffered immeasurable emotional stress each night when he walked out the door to go on duty. No matter how many times he promised he would return home safely and guaranteed that nothing would happen to him, he not only failed to convince his wife, but he also failed to completely convince himself.

"One more year," he kept telling her. "Just one more year and I'll take an office job."

Unfortunately, she didn't have one more year. Undetected cancer slipped in. She died quickly—within two months of the diagnosis.

Distraught by the loss of his wife, Danberg quit his job out of respect for her wishes. He regretted that he hadn't quit soon enough to enjoy his last year with her. He will always blame himself for her premature death.

Cornstalked

He knew that enormous amounts of stress could cause a myriad of health issues. Her years of worrying about him, her sleepless nights watching the clock, holding her breath each time there was a news report on the television or radio about an officer down, all contributed to her shortened life.

He wasn't quite ready for complete retirement. Without a wife, he couldn't deal with the loneliness, so he applied for the sheriff's position in the small town of Grant, Nebraska. His research showed him the crime rate was extremely low and he knew his life wouldn't be on the line each day he went in to work. He still thoroughly enjoyed being a cop. That was until these three hunters mysteriously disappeared.

He sympathized with the women sitting by their phones in Denver, waiting for word that their men were safe. He had watched his wife age, develop cancer, and die from the worrisome waiting.

It would be his job to inform the three women if something catastrophic had happened to their men. Car accidents in the small county had become the most common reason for having to contact family members with the sad news concerning the loss of a loved one.

There might be fewer episodes of being the bearer of bad news in Nebraska, but he still couldn't erase all incidents of that nature from his life simply by leaving California.

It was just past one o'clock in the afternoon, and the snow showed no signs of letting up. That meant, at best, there might be three hours of daylight left. Three short hours of daylight to cover approximately eight hundred and eighty three square miles of sparsely populated farmland, and roads that are not frequently traveled. He could only hope they stayed near a main road and hadn't ventured off on a small, non-maintained, trail road.

His eyes searched the rows of corn as he drove past until he felt himself growing queasy from the motion. He pulled over and called in to Jason. Danberg's eyes and stomach needed a break. He had driven halfway to the county line, eleven more miles to go.

"Tell me what's happening," he said to Jason.

"We have all the surrounding counties doing exactly what you're doing. We're covering all the east and west roads first. No one has spotted the vehicle."

"Good. How many men do we have out from our office?"

"You and two others, Charlie and Fred. Do you need more?"

"I've been watching this snow. We don't have much time until the sun goes down. We might have to contact local farmers and ask for their help. There's an awful lot of miles to cover in such a short amount of time."

"Just let me know when you want me to start calling in more people."

"Why don't you check the map and list the farmers who you think might be helpful down each road. If we could...say...get twenty of them out looking, we can narrow it down more quickly. But don't call them until I tell you," said Danberg.

"Gotcha. I'll get their names and numbers down while I wait for your call."

"I'm assuming you hit a dead end with the family or friends angle?"

"Yep, nothing."

"Okay. Let me know if one of them happens to call home."

"Will do."

CHAPTER 7

Taking one last hopeful glance behind him, the disheartened Danberg eased his car back onto the highway—his being the only visible vehicle on that stretch of the road. As each mile passed without meeting an oncoming car, his concern deepened.

Through the falling snow, he recognized the massive outline of the Venango grain elevators ahead— Venango, the last town squatting on the edge of the state line. If a deputy from Holyoke had followed his instructions, they'd arrive at the state line simultaneously.

The highway, running along the north edge of Venango, does not pass through the town, but skirts the northern boundary of Venango's main street creating a

Cornstalked

"T". The main street consists of a small post office, a tiny café, and two bars.

At the last minute, Danberg cut his steering wheel quickly to the south. His pickup slid out of control into the center of the wide main street—wide enough for cars to park at angles on both sides of the street, and for semis to park in a straight line down the center, allowing traffic to flow smoothly on either side of the semis.

During harvest time, the truckers parked in a long line down the middle of the street while waiting their turn to cross the highway to the grain elevators. At the grain elevator, each driver takes his turn driving over the collection pit to empty his trailer, filled to capacity with either corn or wheat.

Danberg knew the search could be called off if he spotted the Escalade parked anywhere in town. It was a long shot, but he'd feel foolish if he had driven within two blocks of the missing men, and hadn't at least checked.

His hope disintegrated as reality set in. His search came up empty. He hadn't really expected to find them in Venango. They certainly wouldn't be mailing a letter, and it was well past the lunch hour. And, if they wanted to stop at a bar, they most likely would've chosen a bar in Grant, closer to their motel rooms.

When he turned back onto the highway and turned west for a quarter of a mile, he spotted the Colorado Sheriff Department's vehicle parked next to the "*Welcome to Colorado*" sign. He pulled up next to the driver's side and rolled down his window.

The two sheriffs' paths had crossed over the years, but they had no personal friendship outside of work.

"Well?" asked Danberg.

"Nothing. How about you?" asked Sheriff Donald Brewer.

"Nope. How many men do you have out looking?" Danberg asked.

"Just me," came the response. "You think something bad happened to them?"

"Yeah, I do," said Danberg.

"Do you want me to call out more men?" asked Sheriff Brewer.

"Considering the current weather conditions, I think that might be advisable," said Danberg. "Without much time before the sun sets, I'm thinking about calling some of the local farmers to form a search party. That is, if this snow doesn't get much worse. I'd hate to put them in danger of being stranded themselves."

"Hell, most of the farmers are pretty cagey right now, being locked up in the house with their crops still stuck in the field. I'm sure they'd welcome the diversion," said Sheriff Brewer.

"You've got that right," said Danberg.

"I still can't believe this year. We've had more rain than I can remember for one season. The corn's thicker and taller than I've ever seen it, and I've lived here my whole life. More birds this year than ever before, too. And, you know what that means?"

"No, what?" asked Danberg.

"More hunters. More crazy, drinkin', gun totin', city idiots to cause trouble," said Sheriff Brewer.

Danberg nodded his head, "Like the three I'm trying to find."

"Time's not standing still, so we'd better keep moving. I'll call in some reinforcements. Good luck," said Sheriff Brewer.

The two men pulled onto the highway then headed north to the first crossroad where each driver turned back toward the direction of his town.

Danberg called in, "Made my way to the state line. No sign of them. I buzzed through Venango just in case. Anybody call in with any news?"

"Nope. Want me to start calling farmers?" asked Jason.

Danberg drew in a long, deep, breath before saying, "Yeah, go ahead. It's looking ugly out here."

Jason had listed twenty-five farmers who lived on twenty-five different roads, some north and some south of the highway. He instructed them to cruise a five-mile segment of their own roads first, then move over one mile and repeat the process. Stickpins marked the county map on the wall in the Sheriff's department as Jason reached each farmer who agreed to lend a hand in the search.

Jason called Danberg.

"I was able to reach twenty-one farmers," he said. "We should have pretty good coverage before too long. I've had several townspeople stop by to ask about the search for the Escalade. You know how that goes. I'm sure every inch of town has already been searched several times over, and you can bet there'll be twice as many townspeople as farmers out driving around, wanting to be the first one to find the missing vehicle, and hopefully find the three missing men as well."

"At this point, I don't care what it takes as long as we don't spend the rest of the day pulling the search party out of ditches from these damn icy roads," said Danberg. "Keep me informed."

On his way back to town, on a side road, he met three pickups heading west, evidence that most of the residents were out looking for the Escalade. He felt confident they'd find the hunters if they were anywhere inside the county limits.

Jason's line was buzzing with calls. Several red SUVs were spotted, but only a few were Escalades, and out of those only one had Colorado plates. The same one Danberg had stopped earlier in the day.

When the sheriff approached the edge of town, he eased his way through the neighborhoods and weaved through the cross streets, all the while peering toward Central Avenue whenever the opportunity presented itself.

He knew the entire town had been alerted through the gossip chain, and the three men couldn't hide out even if they wanted to. But, just as in Venango, he felt better checking for himself.

Jason called Danberg.

"Morgan, we might have something," said Jason.

"What've you got?" asked Danberg, his adrenaline rising.

"A couple of teenagers spotted a red Escalade, Colorado plates, about seventeen west and four north."

"What about passengers?"

"No sign of them," said Jason.

"Is it locked?"

"Yeah, and there were shotguns inside."

"Shit," said Danberg.

Leaving the shotguns inside the vehicle meant the hunters were not out searching for birds. Something else must have caused them to walk away from their only means of transportation in the cold.

"Tell them to stay in their vehicle," said Danberg. "I don't need them screwing up any tracks that might be out there. I'm on my way."

CHAPTER 8

Danberg called Sheriff Brewer from Holyoke after he turned around to drive west again.

"Brewer, this is Danberg. My dispatcher says they found what could be our missing Escalade."

"Let's hope so," said Sheriff Brewer. "How can I help?"

"I'm not sure if there's anything else you can do, but thanks for the offer. Unless you hear otherwise, hold off on sending out more men. No sense in having a slew of drivers out looking if this one checks out."

"Will do," said Sheriff Brewer. "Any sign of the hunters?"

Cornstalked

"No. That's what worries me," said Danberg. "Their shotguns were found inside the vehicle, but no hunters were spotted."

"Maybe they came with extra guns," said Sheriff Brewer.

"That's what I'm hoping for," said Danberg.

Ordinarily, he would've been able to drive over seventy miles per hour on the old gravel roads, but the ice forced him to proceed far below the legal speed limit of fifty. He was lucky to drive thirty miles per hour in some of the more treacherous spots. But then, some sections of the roads were even worse, and he was resigned to creeping along as slow as fifteen.

Seventeen miles seems to crawl by when you're forced to drive at a fraction of the normal speed limit. Danberg's anxiety mounted.

He focused intently on the dangerous icy patches on the road. He made futile efforts to increase his speed, only to be slowed down again in order to avoid ditching his vehicle alongside the road. Even the four-wheel drive failed to master the treacherous ice, camouflaged by two inches of freshly fallen snow.

His stomach fluttered and churned as if someone poured a full container of slow moving slugs down his throat. His body temperature increased and his pulse quickened. He felt trapped on the road, like in a dream when your legs seem to fail you while you're trying desperately to run away, and you end up going nowhere.

The distance between Danberg's present location and his destination was closing so slowly that, at times, he felt as if his pickup was close to a standstill.

"Damn," he said. "I wonder how the hell those teenagers made it out here on these roads without running off into the ditch?"

He knew they lacked the experience, the quick reflexes, and also the brains necessary to drive safely on icy country roads. But that never stopped them. He had come to dread the frantic phone calls from concerned parents in the middle of the night when their sons or daughters missed curfew.

No matter what the season, the combination of country roads and teenagers, after a drinking party, frequently meant an accident, and unfortunately, often a fatal one.

When he arrived at the scene, the vast number of pickups on the road blocked his view of the red Escalade parked in the shallow ditch, between the road and the cornfield. There were teenagers everywhere—so much for finding tracks or clues.

"What the hell?" he muttered. "Looks like a damn sporting event."

There were kids peering inside the windows and stomping through the snow, destroying any footprints that might have been there offering answers as to which direction the hunters had gone once they left their vehicle.

Although, he didn't expect to see much, considering the accumulation of the snow as the day progressed, it still caused a spike in his temper.

As he stepped out, before joining the curious crowd, he pressed the button on his shoulder radio to tell Jason he was at the scene.

"I finally made it. Hell, there's more kids out here than in the whole town. I'll get back to you," said an angry Danberg.

By that time, Jason had already received the license numbers from the kids who had been the first to discover the missing vehicle. When he ran the plates, he was able to positively confirm that it was registered to Bruce Clarke from Denver, Colorado.

Jason responded, "I ran the plates and it's our missing Escalade. What do you see there?"

"A goddamned mess. There's more teenagers than I first thought. They're everywhere. Hell, they're even running through the cornfield looking for the hunters. I need backup here, and fast."

The crowd that had gathered around the SUV stepped aside to allow Danberg access to the scene. The din of the fast talking crowd subsided as two lines formed, with an aisle down the center for the sheriff. The scene resembled a red carpet approach during the celebrity arrival at the Oscar Awards Banquet.

"Everybody, stand back, please. Go back to your vehicles, but don't leave until we've had a chance to talk to you," barked Danberg.

No one wanted to leave. They stepped back a couple of feet, but they didn't intend to forfeit being in a prime location to watch Danberg perform his formal investigation. Never before had the kids been able to witness a real CSI investigation. They were fascinated.

Danberg spun around to look at them.

"I said, everyone get back in your vehicle!"

This time they moved away, slowly, but they eventually made it to their respective vehicles to wait and watch.

Next, he walked to the edge of the cornfield. The rustle of the leaves from the unpicked corn, and the squeals and laughter from the teenagers running through the rows, infuriated him.

"Everyone, get out of the corn! Now!" he yelled.

His serious tone meant business, and the kids knew he was angry with them, but they still pushed and shoved and giggled their way out. A few of the braver jocks mocked him by imitating his command. Others stepped out peacefully, concerned that they may be in some sort of trouble. All of the teenagers avoided making eye contact with the sheriff when they surfaced at the ends of the rows.

"Get back to your vehicles and wait there until I say you can leave!" he barked again.

Like a wild animal protecting his kill, he stood between the Escalade and the road packed with cars and pickups, his facial expression warning them not to approach.

"Where's my backup?" he called to Jason on his radio.

"They're on their way. Give them another ten minutes. What do you have?"

"Nothing yet. Just the right vehicle, but nothing else. Make sure the guys split up and come in from different directions. If they see any of these kids driving away from here, stop them, and turn them back. I don't want anyone leaving the scene before we've had the opportunity to question them."

"Gotcha."

Charlie and Fred arrived on the scene just as Danberg had requested, one from the north and one from the south. It was actually difficult for them to find a place to park nearby. More cars and pickups had appeared after Danberg's arrival.

The deputies drove down through the ditch to be closer to the Escalade. They stepped from their vehicles and surveyed the crowd. They wondered, like Danberg, how the hell all of those teenagers made the trip from town on icy roads in record time. Fred and Charlie walked straight from their vehicles to Danberg.

Demonstrating his authority over the situation, Danberg instructed his two deputies to interview each and every person on the road. Respecting him during an investigation was an important message for Danberg to convey to the kids. He wanted them to be aware of the difference between bumping into him in town, as the friendly sheriff, and interfering with a potentially criminal investigation.

With his deputies busy gathering information; he turned his focus to the SUV. He intended to take his time to process the scene and attempt to construct a plausible theory in his mind. He refused to allow the onlookers to be privy to his theory, or anything he might discover. Necks strained from the cars and pickups as the passengers continued to watch Danberg's every move.

He returned to his pickup for a camera. He snapped photos of the Escalade and the trampled ground around it. He photographed the interior of the backseat, containing the shotguns. He turned in a full circle, photographing the entire surrounding area.

Sometimes you might catch potential evidence or clues in a photograph that escaped your initial observations at the scene.

Cornstalked

He noticed that two of the shotguns were setting atop their unzipped soft cases, but the third was tossed hastily onto the front seat, pointing toward the passenger door. He made note that there were no keys in the ignition, and the doors were locked.

At this point, he still toyed with the possibility that the hunters had simply run out of fuel and accepted a ride with a friendly farmer or another hunter.

He examined the Escalade thoroughly. Since the SUV obviously wasn't stuck, or damaged in any visible way, he leaned heavily on his first theory, which also included the possibility of engine trouble.

But, if that was the case then why hadn't they shown up in town? Who picked them up and what happened to them?

When he walked around to the front of the Escalade, his eyes were drawn to a broken headlight, and missing paint exposing the gray primer underneath. The spray pattern told him that someone had shot at the vehicle. He squatted down to examine the missing paint more closely. The damage was new, of that he was certain.

He noticed an empty bottle of Jack Daniels on the floor behind the driver's seat, confirming his first suspicion that they'd been drinking. He turned in a complete circle to survey the area, this time with his naked eye rather than through the camera lens.

He checked all four tires as he walked completely around the Escalade—they were in good condition, properly inflated, and still showed adequate tread.

It was obvious they hadn't gone into the cornfield with their shotguns. There were only three shotgun cases in the backseat. So, where the hell were they? And who shot at them? He walked up to the road to check on the interviews in progress. Charlie and Fred moved away from the kids to join him.

"Anything we can use?" Danberg asked.

"Not yet. Most of these kids showed up after the first couple found the SUV. They called their friends and then the party started," said Charlie.

"What do *you* make of it?" asked Fred.

Danberg rubbed his cheek again with his left hand. This time the stubble had broken through the skin, making a scraping sound on the palm of his glove. He looked at the kids, ignorant of the urgency of the situation, then back to the Escalade.

He shook his head, "I'm not sure. The tires are up and the shotguns are still inside. They were definitely drinking. Until we get inside, I can't tell what the gas gauge says. I'd say they ran out of gas and caught a ride to town with someone. But I can't, for the life of me, figure out why they haven't surfaced, except..."

"Except what?" asked a curious Fred.

Cornstalked

"Might be nothing," started Danberg. "But the front end's been sprayed with shotgun pellets. The paint's missing and there's a broken headlight."

"Do you think someone shot at them and forced them out of the vehicle?" asked Fred, as he glanced over at the SUV.

"It's a strong possibility," said Danberg. "I really wish those kids hadn't messed up the scene. It would've been nice to look for tracks in the snow to see how many people were around the vehicle when the hunters got out."

Charlie walked to his car and pulled the keys from the ignition. He walked around to the back and opened the trunk. From the trunk he retrieved a sample straw, used to check diesel cars and pickups, to be certain they're abiding by the law prohibiting them from using farm diesel to fuel their over-the-road diesel vehicles.

He carried it back to the Escalade then he opened the flap cover on the gas tank, unscrewed the cap, and shoved the sample straw deep inside. When he drew it out, it was obvious to the three of them that there was still gasoline in the tank, and more than enough to get them safely to town.

"That blows my fuel theory all to hell," said Danberg. "That leaves engine trouble, or someone forced them out."

"Now what?" asked Fred.

"You two go finish up with those kids, and send them on their way if they don't have anything useful to add. But, make sure you have all their names and cell phone numbers. We might need to talk to them again. Oh, and before you let them go, check their vehicles to see if any of them have a shotgun with them. I want to make sure one of them didn't take a potshot at the Escalade while it was parked here."

The sheriff and the two deputies watched as the last of the kids drove away. What started out as a fun and exciting adventure on a cold, snowy day, soon turned boring and uninteresting while they waited for their turn to be interviewed. The kids were much more anxious to leave the scene than they were to arrive.

"Look at this," said Danberg. He pointed to the ground near the driver's side door. "What do you see?"

"Mud?" said Charlie, not quite sure what Danberg was getting at.

Danberg squatted down as he slowly and carefully brushed away the loose layer of snow.

"Could this be blood?"

CHAPTER 9

Jason called Danberg on the radio. "Do you want me to call the hunters' wives and tell them we found the Escalade?"

Danberg replied, "Let's hold off on that a while longer. I'd rather have some solid information for them about the men first. I'm not sure how they'll take the news that they appear to be missing."

"Okay. I'm going to head home now. Carol's here to take over. I've brought her up to speed on what's going on. She's gonna finish calling the farmers, who are still out looking, and tell them they can go home."

"Hold off on that for now, too. I like the idea of the roads being patrolled in case these guys are on foot. Someone might find them. Tell Carol to give it thirty more minutes then call it off. If they haven't been found on a road by then, it's obvious they're not out walking around, looking for a ride."

"Gotcha."

Charlie had dropped to his knees to get a closer look at the stain on the snow. "Could be blood. Might just be pheasant blood. Might not be blood at all."

"Considering someone shot at the vehicle, let's hope it's not human blood. We could have a homicide on our hands," said Danberg. "Take a sample, and let's send it off to the lab to check it out. I want to be damn sure if it *is* blood, that you're right, and it's just from a bird."

Although the sheriff wanted to be thorough, he also knew not to incite panic in the small town and surrounding counties. Several years earlier, a man named Moses terrorized the sleepy communities of western Nebraska when he went on a killing campaign. He shot one state trooper and one deputy then killed a farmer and stole his pickup.

Every sheriff's department within a one hundred mile radius joined forces to participate in the frightening manhunt. The residents were terror-stricken. Businesses closed early to send their employees home to be with their families.

Everyone avoided going into town for supplies or to do business, preferring to stay close to home. Warnings were broadcast on the radio to remain locked in your home, and not to answer your door unless the person clearly identified himself. The man named Moses was considered armed and dangerous.

Until Danberg had proof that someone had caused harm to the three missing hunters, he didn't want to prematurely alarm the community.

Where to start? Where to start? If they were on foot, which direction had they gone, and why? His eyes scanned the area for anything that might lead him to the path the hunters had taken.

Unfortunately, the kids had completely spoiled any tracks leading in or out of the cornfield. When the hunters left their vehicle, Danberg couldn't tell if they had prowled around the cornfield.

The ice on the road, plus the kid traffic, had ruined any chance of the officers knowing whether or not the three missing men had walked directly to the road, where they may have accepted a ride, or may have been forced into another vehicle.

Suddenly, Danberg realized the snow had stopped after dropping two inches to completely conceal all potential evidence. But, without a thaw before morning, footprints made by the hunters walking along the road will be more visible, and obviously fresh. He turned back to his deputies and watched as they finished their work.

After Fred had collected an adequate sample to be analyzed, Danberg knelt down to brush more snow from the pale, reddish pink stain. The two deputies watched carefully. They never questioned anything Danberg did. Having worked the streets of Los Angeles before he took the sheriff's position, earned him the respect of all who worked beneath him.

They waited. No one spoke.

Finally, Danberg broke the silence. "It's impossible to tell. There's just not much blood here. Maybe a little more than a pheasant's, but then, maybe not, depending upon where the shot hit the bird. Get that sample to town. No sense wasting time speculating over it."

"Should we call a service truck to tow the Escalade to town?" asked Fred.

"Not just yet. Maybe, if we're lucky, they'll come back to it on their own. Hell, maybe they got picked up by some women and were too busy getting laid to come back for it."

Danberg knew better. City people wouldn't leave their vehicles in the middle of nowhere. They are accustomed to living in the city, where any car would be quickly vandalized or stolen if left unattended. And, they certainly wouldn't have left their shotguns behind, in plain sight, inviting someone to break a window to steal them.

Locals don't worry about vandalism, but if you're not from the area, you wouldn't be so trusting. His gut still told him something was not quite right.

"What's next, Morgan?" asked Charlie.

Cornstalked

"Let's split up and talk to everyone who lives up and down this road. See when the last time was someone saw the Escalade drive by."

He knew that in the country, when a car or pickup drives by, everyone stops what they're doing to look up. That's how seldom traffic drives by on the side roads. It's also customary to stop what you're doing and wave at the driver, if you're outdoors. And, that same custom dictates that if you know the family living in the house, and you're friends with that family, to honk your horn as you drive past.

Knowing the storm most likely kept people indoors, he felt confident someone might have watched the strange red SUV drive by, and made a mental note of it.

After a few moments of discussion to plan their questions, the three officers separated to begin their neighborhood interviews.

Fred stopped at the first farm that belonged to Larry and Beverly Stevens. Larry, almost ready to retire, had rented most of his farmland to younger farmers who had studied how to increase yields on fewer acres.

He had sold his livestock several years earlier. Larry and Beverly spend the majority of their time at home, puttering around the house, and watching television.

Larry answered the door.

"Fred, what brings you out here in this weather? Come in, come in," said Larry. "Bev, get Fred a cup of coffee. He looks cold."

Beverly jumped up from her Lazy Boy recliner to rush into the kitchen.

"No, that's okay. I don't have time," said Fred. "I'm just here to ask you a few questions."

"Are you going to ask us about the missing hunters?" asked Beverly.

"Guess you heard," said Fred, not the least bit surprised.

"Yeah, Shirley called me when George went out to help look for them. Did you find them?"

"No, not yet," said Fred. "We found their vehicle. We're assuming someone gave them a ride, and we're trying to find out where they might be."

"How long have they been missing?" asked Larry.

"Since yesterday morning around ten. Well, anyway that's the last time anyone had any contact with them," said Fred.

"I don't believe we saw them at all, in or out of their vehicle," said Larry. "Sorry we couldn't be more helpful. But you know, if they left on foot yesterday, and as cold as it is..."

"Yeah, I know. Chances are they couldn't make it overnight if they were lost outdoors," agreed Fred.

Larry walked Fred to the door.

Cornstalked

Charlie had watched Fred pull into the Stevens farm as he drove past to the next crossroad leading to the Rieger farm.

When Charlie knocked on the door, there was no answer.

Strange, he thought. Where would they be on such a cold evening? He looked in through the garage window and saw both vehicles parked inside. Why were there no lights on and why were both vehicles in the garage? He walked back to the door then turned the knob. It opened. He slowly stepped inside the dark house.

"Anyone here?" he called out.

No answer.

Charlie called Danberg on his radio. "I'm at the Rieger place, and no one's here. There's a pickup and a car parked in the garage. The house is unlocked, but no one responded when I called out. I'm about to search the rooms."

"Don't bother. They're not home. They went with their son and daughter-in-law to Lincoln for a ball game. Guess their son must've drove," said Danberg.

"Should I lock the house when I leave?"

"Nah, they never lock it. They probably don't even have a key to it. Where's your next stop?"

"I thought I'd try Paul Patterson's," replied Charlie.

Danberg had headed south when the three lawmen had separated. He stopped at John and Karen Epp's place.

John and Karen couldn't help much. They both saw the Escalade the morning before, but had nothing new to add.

Charlie stopped at Paul and Liz Patterson's farm. Liz answered the door.

"Hi, Liz. Do you and Paul have a minute to talk?"

"I guess so," said Liz. "Paul's out in the barn doing chores."

"Have you seen a red Escalade driving on your road, either today or yesterday?" he asked.

"No, I don't think so. There just haven't been many people out on the roads with the weather the way it's been. Except for crazy hunters," she responded.

"Okay, thanks. Mind if I go out and talk to Paul?"

"No. Why should I mind? He's in the first barn, the one with the light on. Can I fix a plate for you, we're about to have dinner?"

"No thanks. But, I'll take a rain check. I've got work to do yet tonight," said Charlie.

Charlie made his way through the corral gate, being careful to close it behind him. Paul was feeding his horses when Charlie walked into the barn.

"Hey, Charlie, what are you doing here?" asked Paul in a pleasant voice.

Cornstalked

"Seems we lost a couple of hunters. Have you seen a red Escalade driving around?"

"As a matter of fact I did. They stopped me out on the road yesterday to ask if they could hunt my trees."

"Did they?"

"I told them no," replied Paul.

"What time of day was that?"

"About noon, maybe a little after."

"Did you see which way they went?"

"North."

"Okay, thanks. If you find three guys walking around, will you help them out and give them a lift?" asked Charlie.

"Sure thing," said Paul. "If I see them, I'll make sure to take good care of them."

Charlie had no reason to doubt Paul. After all, Paul was one of the wealthiest, most down-to-earth rancher/farmers in the community.

Paul stepped out of the barn, leaned on the pitchfork he'd been using to bed the stalls, and watched as Charlie drove away.

He had remained cool and calm while he talked with Charlie. He gave Charlie no reason to think he might be lying. No reason at all. But then he *did* tell the truth, the entire truth. It wasn't his fault Charlie failed to ask the right questions.

CHAPTER 10

The previous morning, Friday:

The alarm chirped an annoying sound while a moaning Gayle struggled to find the gray button on the top to stop the incessant noise. She forced one eye open; positive it was too early for her to be dragging herself out of bed to get ready for work.

"Four o'clock, are you out of your mind?" she asked.

Bruce lie beside her, snoring loudly.

"Wake up. Bruce. Wake up," she insisted.

He pulled her close to him. He slowly stroked her naked body.

Cornstalked

She angrily threw his hands away and said, "You set the alarm for four. Did you mean to do that?"

Suddenly, as if she had thrown ice water on him—a thought that had entered her mind—he sat up straight. Rubbing his eyes, he leaned over her to read the red, digital numbers on the alarm clock.

"I've gotta go," he said.

Gayle brushed her long, white blonde hair from her swollen eyes with large bags beneath them. She watched as Bruce climbed out from the bed and started the shower.

"Come join me," he called out from her bathroom.

"No thanks," she said as she rolled over, desperately wanting and needing more sleep.

Bruce had kept her up past midnight. She must make herself presentable for work, and he just had to hang out with his guy buddies on some stupid hunting trip.

"I said, get your ass in here."

The sound of his demands jolted her awake, the same way two cups of black coffee back-to-back in the morning might. She knew all too well not to disagree with him. Not only had she experienced being slapped around by him, on occasion, like he did to his wife, Kimberly, but he also threatened to call in her bank note on her small candle-making shop.

Bruce had helped her open her shop with a loan from his bank when her credit was so bad she couldn't have gotten the loan anywhere else.

She slid her naked body out of bed and slipped into the steaming shower with him.

"That's more like it," he said. "Here, scrub my back."

He handed her the pink, nylon scrubby she hung from the showerhead. Obediently, she scrubbed his back until it glowed a bright pink, applying the pressure just the way he taught her.

He grabbed her and spun her around, trading places with her. He watched as the steaming hot water turned her white flesh pink. He poured shampoo into his palm and lathered his hair, all the while watching her body. He enjoyed watching her face wince from the pain of the hot water, as she succumbed to his orders.

With his hands lathered from the shampoo, he ran them slowly down her body. He repeated his earlier move, tossing her against the wall, as he roughly traded places with her then rinsed the suds from his hair.

She rubbed her upper arms that ached from his grip when he tossed her aside. She couldn't say he didn't know his own strength, because she knew he did.

The once muscular and fit captain of his football team had allowed himself to grow mushy. He sported a potbelly and flabby thighs that were once rock hard from

Cornstalked

hours and hours of football practice. His dark brown eyes required glasses or contact lenses to see beyond his arm's length. He felt the graying hair around his temples, in contrast to his dark brown hair, added to the distinguished look he thought a banker should possess.

Bruce was not the type of man Gayle had dated in the past. She preferred her men to be more physically fit, but he had a financial hold over her that she could not break.

Her forced position as his on-call mistress suited him fine, but sickened her to the point of nausea whenever she saw him or spoke to him.

She planned to drop him the instant she repaid her outstanding loan. Her attempts to switch banks with her loan proved futile with her low credit score. So, she had no choice but to go along with the situation until she could purchase her freedom, like the plantation slaves from the past.

Bruce turned off the shower and opened the door.

"Dry off and meet me in bed," he ordered.

Obediently, she lay on the bed while he grunted on top of her.

"I've gotta go," he said again.

He dressed quickly then walked out the door without turning back to say good-bye.

Gayle rolled over in bed and cried. She wished she never had to see him again.

CHAPTER 11

Bruce tossed his black, designer, overnight bag into the back of his Escalade then climbed in to start the engine. He waited until he felt the cold engine had sufficiently warmed before he left Gayle's apartment complex parking lot and drove directly to the Starbucks around the corner for a hot cup of Espresso Macchiato.

He enjoyed the way the aroma of the hot coffee filled the chilly air inside the SUV. Taking his time before leaving the drive-up window, he lifted the lid for a sip. Did it matter to him that there was a line of customers behind him? Not in the least. After all, this was his first cup of coffee for the morning—he deserved to enjoy it at his leisure.

Cornstalked

A horn honked two cars behind him. He glanced in his rearview mirror, slowly took one more sip, then moved on. Next stop was Rick's house. Not wanting to wait on him, Bruce called him ten minutes before his estimated time of arrival. He didn't care that he might wake Rick's girlfriend, Gina.

Rick answered his cell phone on the second ring, hoping Gina hadn't been disturbed.

"Good morning," said Rick

"Yeah, I guess," said Bruce. "Are you ready?"

"I'm all packed."

"Good. Meet you in your driveway. I don't want to waste any time. We might still get some hunting in if the weather stays bad and we don't screw around instead of getting on the road."

Surprised by the rush in Bruce's voice, Rick answered, "Sure, I'll have everything outside when you get here."

Rick stood in the cold watching the lightly falling snow cling to his luggage. He bounced from one foot to the next. He didn't dare step inside and watch out the window. It was important to him to do whatever it took, on this hunting trip, to convince Bruce that he was the right person to take his place as the bank president, once Bruce moved on to his new position.

Rick wasn't privy to the details of the new position, but he secretly hoped it meant Bruce would also be moving out of the branch office where they currently worked—even if Rick didn't replace him.

Bruce led both Rick and Drew, another co-worker, to believe this hunting trip would help him determine who would be his successor when he moved up the corporate ladder. The three had been planning this trip since the end of summer.

The first week of pheasant hunting in Nebraska had finally arrived. The anxiety and tension between Drew and Rick had been mounting as the weeks progressed, making the working conditions at the office less than optimal. Of course, Bruce did his share to keep the competition alive.

Frequently, Bruce would invite both Rick and Drew to lunch and then stand back to enjoy watching them battle over who would be the first one to pick up the tab.

Bruce even passed a portion of his own workload off onto them, under the guise of teaching them his job. Each man performed his tasks to perfection, actually, better than Bruce himself might have done. Their combined efforts helped cinch the deal for Bruce to be in the running for the new position. The truth was, without them, he might not have had the same opportunity.

Bruce honked his horn as he turned the corner.

Rick gathered his equipment and luggage then rushed to the Escalade to load his gear. Bruce stayed in the driver's seat watching, while Rick made three trips.

Cornstalked

Rick was to supply all of their food for the trip, and Drew, the alcohol. Bruce supplied the ride and, of course, his hunting expertise to help his two novice friends bag their limit.

As they left Rick's neighborhood, Bruce said, "Call Drew. Tell him we're running late. We need him to have his stuff at the curb when we get there."

Rick passed the instructions on to Drew and soon all three men had their supplies loaded and were on their way east for their four-hour drive into Nebraska.

CHAPTER 12

Nebraska:

The cool, crisp, fall air bit the flesh on Paul's weathered face as he stepped outside for morning chores. He drew a deep breath, filling his lungs with that fresh air, holding on to it momentarily, like a smoker taking in the full effect of the nicotine before releasing it.

He reached behind him to be certain he had closed the door, not wanting the cold air to penetrate the warmth of his home. It cost money to keep his large home warm in the cold of winter and he did everything in his power to save a dollar.

Cornstalked

Turning around, his eyes surveyed with pride his hundreds of acres of land, a fair portion filled with horses and cattle, the rest broken from pastureland into farmland. It was an outstanding year for corn production. He stood to make a hefty income from selling his crop after harvest.

Paul, a self-made man, spawned from simple roots, grew his net worth to several million. Not that anyone would notice by his plain bargain-priced rancher attire.

He zipped his old, navy blue vest—filled with polyester fiberfill, no goose down for him. Not only is goose down more expensive but bulkier than he liked. He felt the extra bulk would hamper his dexterity. He watched the zipper as he pulled it toward his neck, being careful not to break the threads holding in the old, worn zipper. His wife, Liz, had warned him that if he brought it to her one more time for repairs she would toss it into the trash.

He rarely bought new clothes, wearing his old shirts until they were threadbare, "more comfortable", he always said. Anyone who spent any time with him soon realized he only owned four work shirts. *Can't wear but one at a time*, his motto.

He buttoned his snug-fitting denim jacket, also showing years of wear, especially around the cuffs where the white threads frayed and hung down around his gloved hands while he fixed fence.

With a brisk pace and a slight jog to his step, he went to the barns to feed his horses. He flipped on the light inside since the sun hadn't risen high enough to shed its morning glow. One bare bulb hung in the center of the six-stall barn. The light bulb did very little to brighten the inside, but adding more light fixtures would be an unnecessary luxury.

The horses could see fine in the dark and Paul knew where everything was, so he didn't need the extra brightness. Besides, there were also six windows, one for each stall, which allowed enough light to enter during daylight hours, removing the need for the one flyspecked light bulb.

His chores began by carefully measuring the correct ratio of corn to oats to feed his horses. He liked to feed a mixture of three parts oats to one part corn. He used an old red and white Folgers coffee tin to make his measurements. He'd been using the same can for thirty years. Probably just as well, since he couldn't replace it easily because he didn't drink coffee at home, only tea. He also didn't drink alcohol. Apple juice, tea, and water were his only liquid choices.

Anyone who came to visit knew those would be the beverages he'd offer, along with an oatmeal cookie or two—unfrosted, of course.

After pouring enough grain to feed six horses into a large, white, plastic bucket he stepped outside. In the center of the corral, he had built feeders from two old tractor tires, stacked one on top of the other, with the heavy boards sandwiched and bolted between them. The horses were safe from injury and could gather around the four-foot wide feeding area, allowing each horse adequate room. No sooner had he poured the grain into the feeder than he heard the pounding sound of hooves coming in from the south pasture.

He watched as the magnificent animals raced toward the corral and through the gate separating the corral from the pasture. Their urgent focus was on their feed bunks. Once inside the corral, they kicked their hind legs high into the air, as a warning to each other, before jogging to an open spot at the feeder.

Dodging the dangerous hooves was second nature to this ex-war veteran who spent his entire life, outside of the war, working with horses and cattle.

He preferred his animals to people, any day. Paul didn't fair well in large crowds, although, everyone he met seemed drawn to him. He preferred his few select friends, actually they were more local neighbors and acquaintances, he didn't really have close friends. That's the way he preferred it.

His soft, blue eyes squinted in the morning sun, exaggerating the deep wrinkles extending out from the corners, as he examined every inch of the animals while they gathered around to feed. Content that everyone appeared to be in good flesh and void of injuries from rough play, he continued on his way.

He had two more corrals of horses to feed then cattle to attend to. While the horses gobbled up their grain, he slipped in among them with three flakes of alfalfa hay and one flake of timothy hay for each feed bunk.

With the horses fed, he turned off the barely visible light, closed the door to the grain room then stepped out of the barn, latching the door behind him. He stomped his feet to shake away the remnants of hay that clung to his clothes—a habit he developed many, many years ago.

He walked back to the house to remove his white, Chevy pickup from the garage. As he backed it out into the driveway and climbed in, he reminisced of the time when his chores were done solely on horseback, but having grown older, he joined the ranks of younger farmers and ranchers using pickups for their daily rounds.

Seated in his generic pickup, waiting for the engine to warm, he tuned the radio channel to Paul Harvey's *The Rest of the Story*. He reached under his seat and pulled out a soft, worn cloth and dusted the dashboard while he listened to the radio. He pampered his pickup much the same way he cared for his livestock. Too bad his wife, Liz, lacked that same respect.

Cornstalked

Liz rarely saw signs of affection from the man who had swept her off of her feet seventeen years earlier. Her transformation to wife and mother caused him to look at her differently, treat her differently, and love her differently. Disappointed, she learned to tolerate the change. She so desperately yearned for the man she married, a man who showed her passion and love.

As the years passed, she grew to understand that the stern tyrant he had for a mother, although he respected her, left him with a bitter feeling toward any woman who reminded him of his childhood years.

In the beginning, she spent a great deal of time with him, feeding the horses, grooming them, and cleaning stalls. He taught her how to ride and she learned well from his instruction.

Paul, an excellent horseman, was also an excellent teacher. He thoroughly understood the mind of a horse. He could anticipate a responses almost before the horse knew it had something to respond to.

He taught her how to read the ears of the horse. They had so much to say. By that one simple rule, the rider should never be unprepared for what the horse might do. For generations, horses have survived with the *flight-not-fight* rule and, at a moment's notice, will jump to the side or take off at full speed, and sometimes both, to avoid danger.

Those ears expressed their thoughts by the position on their head—pinned back against their head for anger, forward because they are focused on or hear something, straight up and moving to search for a reason to jump, or in the forward position, relaxed and floppy, when they're totally calm.

As their years together flew by, it was time to start their family. Paul wanted kids more so than Liz, but she finally gave in to his begging. She gave birth to Peggy. Paul couldn't have been more thrilled.

Liz loved being a mother from the moment she held Peggy in her arms. She quickly forgot the long drawn out months of pregnancy that kept her away from his side, working with the horses and cattle. What she didn't expect was the distance that grew between them after Peggy's birth.

After Liz became a version of his mother, he preferred spending time outdoors with his animals, where he encouraged his daughter to join him at every opportunity. He was a gentle father who loved to teach her everything he knew about the animals. It was his knowledge and care of these animals that had made him a wealthy man.

He drove out from his farmyard, across the road to feed his cattle, yet another part of his routine on an ordinary day. He had no idea how far from ordinary his day would become.

CHAPTER 13

Rick and Drew were forced to listen to the loud and obnoxious rap music that blared throughout the Escalade's sophisticated sound system. Bruce played the beat not just because he enjoyed it, but mostly because he knew how the tone of that style of music annoyed both of his passengers.

For his two underlings the four-hour drive was a boringly gruesome hell. They sighed with relief when they finally approached the Nebraska state line.

"What's the plan?" asked Rick.

"Get drunk and shoot a helluva lot of birds," responded Bruce. " And, don't be hogging that bottle. Hand it over."

Drew, who wasn't much for drinking, especially in the morning, felt ill from the booze sloshing around in his empty stomach. Bruce hadn't offered to pull over for breakfast or any bathroom breaks and they didn't want to ask him for special favors. He made it quite clear from the beginning that he wanted nothing to slow them down. He loved being in control of every aspect of the trip, including when they were allowed to empty their bladders.

As soon as they turned onto the exit ramp from the interstate in Ogallala to head south toward Grant, Bruce found a country road and pulled over to relieve himself.

Rick and Drew quickly jumped out to do the same before Bruce ordered them back inside. He kept stressing time and that they were in a hurry, like he had some sort of deadline or somewhere they needed to be, but he never explained what drove that sense of urgency.

They finally realized how Bruce enjoyed exercising control over them and the situation during their ride. Somehow, with their minds set on pleasing him in anticipation of a job promotion, they missed the control factor that became overwhelmingly apparent on the trip. What kind of person doesn't offer food or bathroom breaks while traveling—an extremely selfish and self-centered person who believes he is superior to those around him.

Twenty miles south of Ogallala, they arrived in Grant. Bruce had made reservations at the Sunsetter Motel. The sign was small and he didn't notice it until they were right up to it. He took the turn into the icy parking lot a little too fast and nearly put his Escalade through the front window of the motel's office.

The three men climbed out and walked toward the office. Rick and Drew stomped the snow from their boots, but Bruce walked in like the owner should be impressed that Bruce chose this motel for his hunting trip, when actually they were just one group of several troops of hunters with the same enthusiasm to be in Nebraska for the first weekend of pheasant season.

"Let's see," said the owner. "You have one double and one single reserved. So I can give you a room with two twins and a room with a queen size. How do you want to be divided?"

"I'll take the queen," said Bruce. "I might be expecting company."

Both Rick and Drew knew he didn't mean Kimberly. They shot questioning glances back and forth. They were aware of Bruce's infidelity, but had no idea he planned to entertain one of his conquests this far from Denver. Or, possibly, he hoped to find some unsuspecting local woman to use and toss aside. Whatever the case, the two men were happy to bunk together and gain a much-needed break from Bruce.

Their rooms were located across the parking lot from each other. Bruce drove to the door of his room and started to unload his things, forcing Rick and Drew to lug their belongings across the icy parking lot while attempting to remain upright, as they slipped and regained their balance along the way.

Once inside their room, both Drew and Rick pulled out their cell phones to call home. Before they could place their calls, however, there was a knock at the door.

Rick opened the door, expecting to see the owner with her arms full of towels, but instead he found an obviously tipsy Bruce standing there.

"Let's go," he said.

"Wait, I want to call Gina," said Rick.

"Not now," said Bruce as he removed the cell phone from Rick's hand. "This trip is all about men, we don't need to be answering to the women. Unless you think you can't handle being so far away from your little lady. Aw...do you miss her already?"

Rick grabbed his cell phone from Bruce and slipped it into his pocket. Drew had already slid his phone into his pocket before Bruce saw him making his call home to Mary. Possibly that move gained him one more point toward becoming the new bank president.

The three men piled into the Escalade and headed west.

CHAPTER 14

Paul, having just finished an early lunch, planned to drive to town, as he did every morning, to have coffee and visit with the other men who gathered for a donut and coffee at the local café. Although he didn't like coffee and rarely finished his cup, he was too macho to request a cup of tea in front of the others.

He was running late. He had missed the mid-morning crowd, but knew he'd catch them over the lunch hour. He put on his jacket and hat. Then he pulled his heavier, warmer, light tan coat from the hook to take along in the event he had to change a tire or help pull someone from the ditch along the side of the road. He had learned to deal with the cold, blustery weather by always being prepared.

Patricia Bremmer

He whistled softly to himself, a habit he had developed long ago as a stress release. He eased the pickup along the lengthy driveway to the road's edge. He hesitated when he noticed a bright red Escalade slowly approaching.

Hunters, he thought. He didn't have much use for hunters. He had long ago given up his desire to kill animals. When he was a boy, he hunted every time the opportunity presented itself. Sometimes he'd finish his chores and stay out past dusk with his dogs and horse.

During the war, his exposure to death had changed him. He left an innocent farm boy, having never been to a city, nor experienced the dangers that went along with the dark streets and dark-natured people who walked them.

He had learned to fight the elements of Mother Nature but had to be taught, as an adult, how to fight man against man. He was whisked away from the safety of his small, rural community where everyone was his friend, and shipped to a strange land where he was turned into a soldier, a man who was forced to kill or be killed.

He returned two years later no longer a boy, but a grown man with a new view on the value of a human life.

The shiny, SUV, now splattered with frozen slush from the town streets and the deicer that caused them to thaw, mixed with the snow from the country roads, eased to a stop.

Cornstalked

Paul watched as a young man in his early thirties, literally dressed to kill, stepped out to speak to him.

He always wondered why city hunters thought they needed to spend hundreds of dollars on bulky, camouflaged clothing, with heavy boots—making walking more difficult and increasing fatigue more quickly—orange vests, and matching orange stocking-knit hats.

When he was a young boy, he rode bareback and barefoot while he hunted jackrabbits and cottontails. The skin on his feet toughened into flesh-toned leather during the summer months when the only reason to wear shoes was to go into town or to attend church services on Sundays.

There was an old woman, nicknamed Bloody Mary, who lived alone and paid the local farm boys fifty cents for every rabbit they brought to her.

On a good day, Paul could make over ten dollars. Rabbits were plentiful; actually more than plentiful, they had reached nearly plague levels, destroying crops, and reducing the income the farmers needed to earn from those crops. The farmers were happy to let their sons slip away, whenever the notion struck them, to keep the rabbit population down.

Paul rolled down his window to hear what the eager stranger had to say.

"Excuse me, sir. Would you mind if we hunted your trees?" asked Bruce, showing his perfect smile—recently whitened.

"I'd rather you didn't," came the response from Paul, his voice so soft the words were barely audible.

"You say, you'd rather we didn't?" asked the hunter, thinking he might have misunderstood him.

Bruce had just spotted at least two-dozen birds in Paul's trees. Surely this guy wasn't keeping them all for himself.

"That's right," Paul cleared his throat. "I'd rather you didn't."

"Can I ask why?" persisted the young man.

"I have horses and cattle and I don't want anyone getting hurt from an accident."

"I can guarantee you won't have anything to worry about," said the hunter smugly.

"That's right, I won't," murmured Paul, "because you're not hunting on my property."

He rolled up his window, pulled onto the road, and drove north out of the hunters' view.

CHAPTER 15

Feeling angry and defeated, Bruce kicked his hunting boot into the snow on the gravel road as he gnawed at the flesh on the inside of his lower lip. With his position as president of his bank in Denver for the past several years, he was unaccustomed to anyone standing up to him or disagreeing with his decisions.

His, *the world owes me,* attitude developed at a young age. During his high school years, the leadership role he took on fit him well, starting with the position of captain of the football team. Smart, good-looking, charismatic, and above all, a very competent athlete, he was the perfect choice.

Everyone, including the teachers and staff, looked up to him as the school celebrity. Unwarranted special attention would make it difficult for any teenager to keep his ego in check. His team members followed his lead from one victory to the next, feeding his already over-inflated ego. He learned to strut his stuff and expected everyone to bend to his every wish, which, unfortunately, they did.

When he started dating Kimberly, she felt she was the luckiest person in the world. As a cheerleader, she was able to cheer him on at every game. It was *her* boyfriend who led the school team to the state finals.

He was a senior and she was a junior when they began dating. It broke her heart when he went away to college. She refused to date anyone while he was away, at his request for her to remain faithful to him. Meanwhile, he partied hard at college, using every girl he managed to get drunk.

Although Bruce played a little college football, he never made it to leadership status, then an injury his second year put an end to his career as a football star. That injury also offered him a convenient excuse to maintain his pride by convincing everyone back home that, had it not been for the injury, he *would* have been a star player.

You could say that injury saved him, allowing him to continue to feed his ego. After graduation, he landed a job at the bank strictly because of his reputation in high school and his father's connections. His grades at school couldn't land him a high paying job without a glowing recommendation.

When he returned to Denver from his college days, at Colorado State University in Fort Collins, he soon discovered that his friends had scattered across the country. Those who had remained in Denver had married and started their families. Marriage, a family, and working to make ends meet caused them to grow up in a way that was totally foreign to Bruce with his immature ways.

No one seemed to care much about his high school glory days as a star jock any longer, no one else except for Kimberly. She had gone away to college and was no longer pining away for him in Denver.

During her Christmas break, she drove home to spend time with her family. He had hoped she would come back for the holiday. He tried to find out from her parents where she had gone to college and how to reach her, but they ignored his calls. They hoped the years and distance would cause her feelings for him to diminish. Her parents, being older and wiser, could see Bruce's true character, and he was not their first choice for their daughter.

Through friends, he managed to make a connection with her. Much to the disappointment of her parents, she was more than willing to pick up their relationship where it had left off when he went away to college. By rekindling their romance, she was able to feed his malnourished ego.

Bruce needed her to sustain his high. He convinced her to drop out of school to become his wife. She learned early on in their marriage that he was not the man she had bargained for. His showy ways of flowering her with gifts and dinners at lavish restaurants—always his choice—changed into a demanding and degrading husband.

When the flowers stopped coming, she also found herself spending more time at home, alone. He refused to allow her to work outside the home. He thought it diminished his image as a successful businessman to have a working wife.

Her attempts to go against his wishes were futile. He'd find a way to sabotage every job she had by making her late or call in sick, if he needed her to run errands for him. Finally, she gave in and just let him have his way. She became a full-time housewife, a full-time servant to her husband, the king.

Next, he wanted kids, and lots of them. She tried to get pregnant, but one night during an argument over a wrinkled shirt that she had forgotten to iron, he slapped her. He slapped her so hard that she fell back against the hall mirror, requiring twenty-two stitches in her scalp.

Her family and friends had no idea what he did behind closed doors and thus began the routine beatings.

Cornstalked

Under no circumstances was she going to bring a child, or children, into their dangerous home with his uncontrollable temper.

Avoiding sex with him was not an option. She feared the repercussions of his discovery that she was taking birth control pills, so she opted for a birth control implant. He never knew about her choice, and she was always careful to pay only with cash. She found a clinic outside of their Denver area, one where there was no chance he'd drive by and spot her parked car.

Nobody stood up to Bruce, nobody until this mild-mannered, old farmer, Paul.

Bruce felt reluctant to return, defeated, to the SUV and his friends.

"Did he tell you no?" asked Rick through his open window.

"Yeah, the old goat wants to keep all the birds to himself."

"Where should we go from here?" asked Drew, who had taken over the driving. He leaned forward over the steering wheel to hear Bruce's response.

Bruce walked alongside the SUV, kicking the tires and thinking. He turned toward Paul's house and relieved himself in the snow covering the road, marking his territory, signaling the fight was on.

He took longer than necessary, not wanting to return to the Escalade without a plan. He glanced north in the direction Paul had driven then toward the south. No one else was on the road but the three of them.

He continued to stare through the trees at the white house, set back three hundred feet from the road. He watched the horses playing in the pasture south of the house. He chewed the inside of his lip once again.

The sound of several pheasants flapping their wings and cackling as they flew to join the others in the trees behind Paul's house turned his attention away from the house and the horses.

He zipped his jeans then turned quickly toward the other men.

"You know what? To hell with him. He doesn't own those birds. Who in the hell does he think he is? Pull around behind the house and let's walk those trees."

The two men in the Escalade didn't dare question Bruce's decision. They backed the vehicle down the gravel road until they came to the intersection of a trail road and the main road. With trees lining both sides of the trail, they felt confident they were completely hidden from view.

There was a break in the clouds and the sun shone brightly on the crusted snow, creating a glare that required sunglasses to protect their eyes from the burn.

Bruce was back in charge. They climbed out. The three men gathered around the back of the Escalade and passed around their bottle of Jack Daniels before starting the trek through the trees.

Cornstalked

Spending most of their time in offices at the bank hadn't prepared them for the cold temperatures they faced outside the warmth of the vehicle. Being slightly overweight from lack of exercise, their bellies extending over their belt lines forced them to buy coats slightly larger than their frames required, just to cover them, which made walking more difficult.

The bottle made one more round before they ventured into the tree row. Armed with their shotguns and booze, they began their hunt—man against beast, in this case, the pheasants played the role of beast.

Over the years, many storms had caused the tired, old, elm trees to shed branches. The decaying wood created thick underbrush that made perfect cover for pheasants and other small wildlife.

Paul was the only one who used that trail road. He had a water tank in the adjacent pasture, a gate at the end of that road led into his pasture. If he didn't jog to the tank from the house, he'd drive out to be certain the horses living in that pasture had adequate water. Paul hadn't made the drive since the recent snowfall. The drifts were too deep.

The three men, unaccustomed to the drifted terrain, soon learned that the weight of each step pushed their boots through the snow and snapped branches buried beneath, alerting the nearby pheasants who immediately took flight away from the hunters.

Several birds flew up from only three feet away. The startled men raised their shotguns and fired. The sound echoed through the trees and they watched as several more birds took flight well out of range for the inexperienced hunters to even consider shooting.

Rick suggested, "Maybe we should walk the trail road to the end and then turn around and walk the trees, sending the birds closer to the Escalade. That way, when we hit the birds we won't have as far to carry them."

Anything to avoid excess exercise, the others agreed.

Trudging along the path, they found themselves breathlessly struggling to advance in the deep snow. The trees had done their job as windbreaks, catching the snow and holding it back away from the house, creating drifts sometimes three feet deep.

At the end of the trail road, they stopped to rest.

"Man, I should've been spending more time in the gym," said Drew.

"Oh stop your whining, you wuss," said Bruce, grateful for the break.

He was breathing even harder than his two companions, although he'd be the last to admit it. They leaned against trees for support, when they really would have preferred sitting, but there was no place to accommodate them in the snow.

Cornstalked

Looking back, they realized they had only walked less than half of a mile. Hot, sweating, and out of breath, they still had to return to where they had begun, only this time they had to be prepared to react quickly to drop the birds as they flushed them from their cover.

Drew feared Bruce might have a heart attack, right there in the middle of nowhere, the way his breathing sounded. He took it upon himself to be responsible for extending their little break.

"I need a drink. How about you?" asked Drew.

"Sounds good to me," said Bruce.

"Yeah, sure," agreed Rick.

Drew took off his backpack and removed the bottle of Jack Daniels. He took a small drink then passed it to Bruce.

Bruce took a big slug. Their little walk had left Bruce hot and thirsty on this cold day. His overheated condition came about partly because he was still angry about Paul's rude response to his request, partly because the sun soaked into his heavy clothing, and partly because he was so dreadfully unfit.

With only beef jerky for breakfast, and several hours of swigging on the now half-empty bottle of whiskey, the effects of the alcohol became more apparent. When they stood to leave, their balance faltered from the combination of the booze and the fatigue from struggling through the snow.

"Maybe we should head back to town for lunch and come back out later," suggested Rick.

"Are you out of your mind? We came here to hunt, and we're gonna hunt the old man's trees and take home the old man's birds. Are you with me or not?" asked Bruce.

"We're with you," said Drew. "Which way do you want to go?"

"Well, asshole. If we walked up the road to avoid the pheasants, don't you think we should walk in the trees to return?"

Drew and Rick exchanged glances. They knew they'd better get some food into Bruce before the alcohol completely took over his mind.

"Follow me," slurred Bruce.

They moved into the thick underbrush of the trees and headed back. Birds took flight all around them. They shot carelessly into the air, missing every bird.

The sound of the branches cracking from the pellets exploding from the shotgun shells filled the air. They continued east toward their vehicle. When they were only fifty feet from the Escalade, a flock of birds took to the air again. They fired.

"I got one!" yelled Bruce.

"Me, too," said Rick excitedly.

They ran clumsily in the directions the birds had fallen.

Cornstalked

When they reached the SUV along the way, Bruce groaned, "One of you bastards hit my Escalade. Look at it."

The front end sported a broken headlight and the spray of pellets had chipped the shiny, red paint, exposing the drab, gray primer.

"I'm going after my bird," said Rick as he darted through the trees and over the fence into the rancher's corrals.

"I can't find it!" he yelled.

The other two joined him. They wandered through the corrals looking for the downed birds within clear view of the house.

CHAPTER 16

Peggy called out, "Mom, hurry! I think there's hunters in with the horses!"

Liz rushed to the window. She had hoped Peggy was mistaken, but she wasn't.

Suddenly, several of the horses burst into the corral, running at full speed, bucking and playing, hoping the drunken humans were about to feed them again.

The men darted for the safety of the white post-and-rail corral fences, stumbling and falling along the way. Bruce rolled over onto his back, raised his shotgun, and took aim at one of the horses racing toward him.

Liz and Peggy held their breath. They turned away, waiting for the horrible sound of one of their prized animals being shot by the trespasser. Liz knew there wasn't time to run out and try to stop them.

The horse pivoted and turned away at the last second.

"Call Dad," cried Peggy.

"I can't. My phone's in my purse and my purse is in the car next to the corral fence."

It was just the previous month that Paul had convinced Liz to drop their landline and go strictly with their cell phones. How she dreaded that financial decision, especially since they could easily afford several landlines.

Terror gripped the two when they realized they were alone on the property with three strange men, armed with shotguns, who appeared to be intoxicated.

All they could do was watch and wait. Damn, why hadn't they bought Peggy a phone of her own?

The men climbed over the fence then dropped to the ground on the other side, laughing at their near escape from the deadly horses. Once again, they passed around the bottle.

By then, all three of them were silly drunk. Drew and Rick had lost all sense of control.

Bruce faced the house and, as he tipped back his head for the last swallow, he noticed the figures of two women standing near the window, watching helplessly.

Instantly, he knew they must be that old goat's wife and daughter.

"Hey, boys, take a gander at the babes. Wanna have a little fun?"

"Hell, why not?" said Rick, not quite knowing what Bruce had in mind.

"What's going on?" asked Drew.

"Look," said Bruce. "Don't you think they look a little lonely?"

Drew looked toward the house. He saw Liz, actually quite beautiful, who had a daughter to match. Both had long, black hair draping over their narrow shoulders onto their petite frames. Peggy carried slightly more body weight than her mother, but just enough to give her a sexier figure.

Bruce studied both women, his eyes roaming the length of their bodies as they stood in front of the large picture window, overlooking the driveway. He decided the smaller of the two must be the old man's wife.

"Hell, I'll bet that old man can't keep her happy," slurred Bruce. "Come on."

The men rose awkwardly from the ground, the lack of food and the abundance of alcohol had relieved them of their decision-making abilities. Their minds dulled, making them obedient to the demands and suggestions blurted out by Bruce. Once balanced on their feet, they ran toward the house where the frightened women stood frozen and watching.

With the butts of the shotguns balanced on their hips, they slid shells into the holding chambers while the women watched in fear, with nowhere to run, and no means to call for help.

Surrounding the house, shooting into the air and laughing, the men searched for an open door. Breaking a window would allow them access to the women if the doors resisted them. How far would they go? What was the extent of control Bruce had over his companions? Would they willingly attack and rape innocent women simply by Bruce's goading?

After they finished with the women, they stumbled back through the trees, found their Escalade, and drove away, still in a drunken stupor.

Seconds after they pulled onto the road, they met Paul returning home. They honked, waved, and saluted him.

"Drunken city bastards," he said in his soft tone.

Paul assumed they had defied him by hunting in his trees. His eyes slowly scanned the corrals, searching for any sign of an injured horse. The red shell casing on his driveway, contrasted by the bright white snow, caught his eye. No longer needing to assume, Paul knew not only had they hunted his trees, but they also had the unmitigated gall to stand in his yard to reload their shotguns. He rushed inside.

Liz and Peggy ran to his arms for comfort and protection.

They could barely speak through their sobs.

"What happened?" he asked, his quiet voice had grown firm.

"Those men, oh Paul, what they did to us!" said Liz.

"What'd they do?"

"Peggy, go to your room and don't come out until I tell you," said Liz.

Liz might have ordered Peggy out of the room, but she disobeyed her mother and hid behind the door. She listened as her mother struggled to find the words she needed to describe how the three men had broken into the house and violently assaulted them. She stopped to start her story again, still lacking the words to invoke sympathy from her already angry husband.

"Are you going to tell me what happened or not?" asked Paul.

"Isn't it obvious what they did to us? Do you really need to hear all the nasty details from me?"

"I said, tell me what happened," Paul repeated, still not wanting to believe the thoughts racing through his mind.

Cornstalked

"It wasn't too long after you left, Peggy looked out the window and saw three hunters in the corrals with the horses," Liz began.

Instantly, he spun his head around to look out the picture window at the corral. He envisioned the scene the women had witnessed.

"Go on," he urged.

"We saw one of them raise his gun to shoot one of the horses."

"Did you try to stop them?"

"We were afraid."

"Afraid of what?"

"Good grief, Paul, there were three drunken men out there with guns, and all you can think about is why we didn't try to protect your precious horses?"

"So what happened next?"

Liz looked around the room to be certain Peggy hadn't returned.

"They saw us watching them from the window."

"Why didn't you call me, or one of the neighbors, or the sheriff, for God's sake?"

"I couldn't. My phone was in my purse and my purse was in the car in the driveway. I pulled it out after you left. We were thinking about driving to town. Then Peggy saw the men."

"So they saw you, and then what?"

"They finished whatever it was they were drinking and loaded their guns in front of us. Then..." she started to cry. "Then, they ran around the house checking the doors and shooting their guns."

"Did they get inside?"

By now Liz was even more emotional. She couldn't tell if Paul felt anger with her for not stopping the men, or if he was mad because of her phone being in the car, or that his horses could have been injured or killed. Not knowing the true reason for his anger, Liz became angry with Paul.

"I'm not going any further. You know exactly what happened. They came in, they attacked us, and they left."

"By attack, do you mean...?"

"What do you think I mean?"

"Peggy, too?" he asked.

"You saw how shook up she was. She wasn't crying for nothing."

He pulled away from Liz, not quite knowing how to deal with an emotional female and her tears. He stepped back and examined her tear-stained face and then his gaze covered her clothed body, looking for signs of the assault.

"You don't look like you're hurt too bad. You'll be fine," he said as he walked out to the barn to check his horses.

Cornstalked

Liz couldn't believe her ears, or her eyes. She watched him walk out the door then she stormed off to her bedroom to cry.

Paul found two dead pheasants in the weeds under the corral fence. He carried the limp bodies to his pickup and tossed them into the back then he climbed in and drove away.

CHAPTER 17

Paul cruised angrily down the country roads with no destination in mind. How far would he drive? How far should he drive? What would it take to calm him? His grip tightened on the steering wheel as he felt his pulse throbbing in his head. It had been a long time since he felt such intense animosity toward another human being.

Removing himself from the painful situation at home was necessary. He needed time to clear his mind and ponder the story Liz had shared with him. Had she called him before he returned home, before he met the drunken slobs on the road, he might have turned his pickup around and followed them. What happened next could've resulted in someone getting hurt. Standing up to three, drunken, armed men, he might have been the one experiencing the most pain.

He often said if he were ever to commit a serious crime, if the opportunity arose when he had to kill someone to defend himself or his home, he would buy a bottle of whiskey first and drink it until he was sloppy drunk.

Since he didn't drink—ever—he felt certain he could use the fact that he was under the influence to aid in his defense.

The thought to call the sheriff and turn in the drunken, lunatic hunters crossed his mind. But then what? Their word against his wife and daughter's?

Paul was a very private man, and didn't want the neighbors to discuss what had happened to his wife and daughter. He knew the stories would spread across the county at record speed. Everywhere Peggy or Liz, or even he, for that matter, would go they would be subjected to stares and whispering behind their backs.

And then, since the men were drunk, would that excuse them in a court of law? Would the very plan he saved for an emergency alibi be the same reason they might be exonerated?

His mind raced with a variety of scenarios. His thoughts returned to Liz and Peggy. Should he go home to sit down and talk it over with them? Should he explain to them how important it is that the incident remains a secret? He had lived in the county his entire life; he knew what ruthless gossip would do to their reputations. How could he get them to understand?

Paul continued to cruise down the country roads for the better part of an hour before he spotted the red Escalade parked along the edge of a cornfield, less than a quarter of a mile down the road.

He felt his pulse quicken. He glanced in his rearview mirror and saw no one else on the road. He looked forward as far as he could see, which sometimes, on country roads, could be well beyond a mile.

He tried to control his breathing by drawing in deep breaths, but it didn't help. His anger mounted at the sight of them. He wanted to tear them apart with his bare hands.

Paul needed to calm himself. He still had his reputation to uphold. How would it look to the community if he let his temper get the best of him? Although the neighbors would agree with his motives, the story of him losing his temper and attacking the men would be how they would remember him for the remainder of his life. Was he willing to sacrifice his family's reputation to seek revenge on those low lifes from the city?

Rick leaned against the SUV while Bruce and Drew had gone deep into the rows to frighten the birds out toward Rick, who hoped to quickly drop his limit.

Cornstalked

Paul drove past, while the drunken Rick, not recognizing him, waved. Paul checked the road one last time for a sign of neighbors or hunters then pulled onto a maintenance road leading to the center pivot of the sprinkler system used for watering the corn crop.

He felt calm. He felt in control. His breathing had returned to normal. He slowly and methodically slipped out of his pickup, tipped the seat forward, and removed his always-loaded .22-caliber rifle. He rested the rifle against the rear driver's side tire.

Next, he removed the coat he was wearing, the lightweight, denim jacket wouldn't provide him the insulation he needed against the cold air. He slipped his arms into the light tan coat, the length of which hung just below his hips. Ever so slowly, he silently closed the door to his pickup.

After adjusting his hat tighter onto his head and zipping his jacket, he slipped on the rubber boot covers he carried in the back of his pickup. He hated to ruin a good pair of leather Red Wing boots by getting them wet in the snow.

He walked just inside the outermost row of corn until Rick's profile came into view. Easing his way toward the man instinctively brought back Paul's training as a soldier. The training that changed a mild-mannered country boy, whose only purpose in life was to ride his horses and hunt rabbits, pheasants, and coyotes. The training that turned each soldier into a killer with no remorse. The training that sent those soldiers home with no means to decompress after fighting hand-to-hand combat.

Paul silently and skillfully approached Rick without being seen or heard. He raised his rifle and fired, dropping the unsuspecting hunter with one clean shot to the heart.

CHAPTER 18

Bruce and Drew had barely walked fifty feet into the corn when they heard the unexpected gunshot.

"What the hell," said Bruce. "We're too close for him to be shooting into the corn. I hope to hell he was shooting off in another direction or aiming up. Stupid bastard's gonna get us killed."

"I, for one, hope he got a bird. I'm cold and hungry," said Drew.

"I can't believe you two pansy asses. I thought you wanted to hunt, and all I get out of both of you are complaints."

"Now, wait one minute. We haven't complained about one damned thing. We've gone along with everything you wanted."

"Yeah, yeah," said Bruce. "Whatever."

"Whatever, hell. No job's worth this," said Drew.

"I guess that means you're no longer in the running for the promotion?"

"Not if it means I'm going to get frostbite or shot by an overanxious, drunken co-worker."

"See you *are* complaining," said Bruce.

"Right, I guess I am. Maybe I don't like the way you try to control every situation. You told us to keep our mouths shut about your little fling last night. I don't appreciate lying to my wife about your affairs."

"You don't have to lie, just don't say anything," said Bruce. "It's not like she's going to bring it up. I can't picture her asking you where Bruce spent the night, can you?" asked Bruce.

"She might not have come right out and asked, but I still felt like I was keeping something from her."

"See, you *can* make your own choices," said Bruce.

"Oh really? I didn't think it was my choice to go without a hot breakfast this morning just so we could get here an hour sooner. I don't think it was my choice not to call my wife, and I don't think it was my choice to torture those women earlier today."

"So that's what's really bothering you?" said Bruce. "No stomach for a little fun once in a while?"

"That's not my idea of fun," said Drew.

Cornstalked

"Well, when I get word about my five o'clock phone call from Kimberly, I guess I can let Rick know he has the position."

"Fine with me. Hell, let's just go tell him right now," said Drew. "I want to go back to town and take a hot shower and get a hot meal and call my hot wife. I plan to stay in my room until we head back to Denver, no more of this freeze-your-ass-off hunting trip for me."

"You've got fire in your gut. Too bad I didn't see it sooner. You would've made a good president. But no one talks to me the way you just did. Do you understand me? No one," said Bruce. "As a matter of fact, when we get back to Denver you can clear out your desk. I'm firing you."

"So, you think you can haul my ass out here on this weekend outing and fire me for personal reasons without proper office protocol? I'll take it up with the board. It might be your sorry ass that gets booted out."

"Don't count on it, buddy," said Bruce.

Drew shoved Bruce aside as he passed him to head back to the Escalade.

Bruce hung back, refusing to walk with him. Then it occurred to him that he might give his version of the story to Rick before Bruce had the opportunity to explain his side.

Besides, he wanted to be the one to give Rick the news about being the chosen one. He wanted to be the first to congratulate him, and in the process, make absolutely certain he would back him with his decision to fire Drew.

The cornstalks were tall, standing well over the heads of the men. Since they were hunting in irrigated corn, the rows were also much closer together. The entire field was more dense than dryland corn, making walking more challenging, and impossible for the two men to stay shoulder to shoulder inside of a row, which was actually fine with Bruce. He stepped sideways through the cornstalks to the adjacent row then sped up his pace in the furrow between the rows to catch up to Drew.

Drew looked through the leaves at Bruce, who refused to look back at him. Drew continued marching forward, stumbling on the concealed ruts and ridges buried beneath the snow.

They had parked the Escalade approximately thirty feet from where they had argued and parted ways. They walked in silence. Twenty feet to go and the pace picked up. Ten, and the red color from the Escalade peeked through the tan leaves—they were almost there.

What they saw ahead of them, down the row, stopped them dead in their tracks. They felt their hearts beating hard in their chests as they watched Paul drag the lifeless body of their fellow hunter into the corn.

"What the hell?" said Bruce.

"Shhh," said Drew.

Cornstalked

"That stupid hunter must've shot Rick by accident. We've got to go stop him from getting away," said Bruce.

Bruce lived his life by pushing people just short of their limit of patience, gauging just how far he could stretch the tension line for future reference. He refused to cut anyone any slack. He felt justified in pointing out every mistake anyone else ever made while refusing to take any criticism for his own words or actions. The accidental shooting of Rick was not to go unpunished, he would see to that.

Bruce's determination showed in his movement the last eight feet to the mournful scene he and Drew had witnessed.

"Wait," whispered Drew.

"What the hell for?" asked Bruce.

"Shhh. He'll hear you," said Drew.

"I don't give a damn if he does. He's not going to get away with it."

Bruce took one more unwavering step forward. The sound of the nearby dried leaves rustling caused Paul to turn toward Bruce and Drew.

Drew put his hand on Bruce's shoulder to stop him.

"Just wait a minute, will you," Drew whispered.

Bruce, still angry with Drew, was about to speak in response when Drew slipped his gloved hand over Bruce's mouth.

"Look at that man. Isn't he that woman's husband?" asked Drew, not wanting to release his hold on Bruce until he was certain he understood the potential severity of the situation.

Bruce quickly played back the dozens of married women with whom he'd had affairs. Realizing not one of them would be sharing a cornfield on a hunting trip with him, he let the list melt from his mind.

Bruce removed Drew's hand from his mouth and turned to face him. He mouthed the words, "You mean the guy who didn't want us to hunt his trees?"

"Yes," whispered Drew.

They stopped moving forward and remained frozen in place. Holding their breath, they watched as Paul returned to their Escalade, removed the keys, and locked the doors.

"What the hell," whispered Bruce. "That bastard's crazy."

For some insane reason, they felt that if they remained motionless Paul wouldn't see them. Paralyzed and horror-stricken, they watched in disbelief.

CHAPTER 19

Paul threw his shoulders back and stood tall. He adjusted his hat and tugged at his jacket while he scanned the empty road in both directions then moved silently into the cornfield.

His soft blue eyes had transformed into a steely gray and they looked directly at Drew and Bruce. His cold, piercing eyes focused on their faces as if he could look right through them.

No longer paralyzed by fear, but rather forced into action by that fear, the two frightened hunters scrambled out of view. They tried to cross the rows of corn without drawing Paul's attention, but the high ridges and deep snow caused them to stumble and fall, breaking cornstalks, or causing them to rustle and sway, alerting a keen eye to their location.

Paul had a keen eye, complimented by his keen hearing. Having spent most of his life in the country maneuvering cornfields in the crisp fall weather in search of birds or coyotes, his gait remained smooth and steady.

With their eyes wide open, rapidly scanning the rows of cornstalks for any sign of movement, the hunters stopped and squatted back-to-back, hoping to avoid the madman.

Afraid to move a muscle, or to even allow their chest cavities to fully expand to take in air, they took frequent, shallow breaths while they watched and listened.

Suddenly, Drew realized even their short breaths, when exhaled, released a smoke signal that rose above the stalks as the cold outside air met their hot breath.

Drew tapped Bruce on the shoulder. Bruce, without saying a word, turned to face him. Like a scene from an underwater movie when the divers, unable to speak, could only communicate by using hand or eye signals, the two hunters attempted to convey their thoughts.

While Bruce looked into Drew's face, Drew released a breath and pointed to the rising vapor. Bruce nodded, expressing he understood.

After each inhalation, they pulled open their jacket collars and exhaled slowly into the cloth. Concentrating on their breathing took their focus momentarily away from plotting their escape route.

Once they felt they had a safer exhalation rhythm down, they needed to formulate a plan, not just any plan, but a well-thought-out plan to save their lives.

Drew fashioned his fist into a make-believe gun like all little boys used while playing cops and robbers, or cowboys and Indians, or pretend army battles.

Bruce furrowed his brow and tipped his head, puzzled at the message Drew attempted to relay.

Drew used his other hand to point, first at his fist-formed gun and then to point out into the cornfield, signifying Paul.

They were both aware that calling out to each other or even speaking in a low whisper might be enough to alert Paul to their exact location and inevitably lead to their death.

Bruce looked around them then turned to Drew and raised his hands, palms up, elbows close to his body, signing, *now what?*

Bruce, who had an answer for everything and refused to admit he was wrong or out of control of any situation, turned to Drew for advice. The animosity that had mounted between them only moments before had been replaced by camaraderie rooted in survival.

Drew simply shook his head, indicating he had no answer to their deadly dilemma.

The two men remained motionless, breathing in the cold air, exhaling the warm air into their clothes, and waited. They didn't know why they were waiting, but somehow sitting still made them feel safe. But how long could they stay in one spot before Paul would stumble upon them?

Should they make their way back to the road and hope for someone to drive by, offering assistance? Would Paul soon tire of the search and return home without harming them?

A million scenarios of escape or death darted in and out of their thoughts. Not one thought stayed long enough to forge a feasible plan.

Drew heard Bruce draw in a deep breath and hold it. He whipped his head around quickly, first to his right and then to his left. He stopped when he saw what had caused Bruce to gasp.

They caught their first glimpse of Paul stalking them. He was a mere six feet away. Still hidden by several rows of corn, the two men, slowly and without a sound, lowered themselves to the ground. They flattened their bodies, pressing down hard onto the snow-covered furrow.

They experienced an overwhelming urge to close their eyes like a young child attempting to hide. Somehow, not seeing what surrounds you lends to the feeling of invisibility. But that gut-wrenching fear of the unknown forced them to keep their searching eyes wide open.

Their breathing had all but stopped completely, not wanting to allow telltale vapors to rise. Their hearts beat hard inside the cavity of their chests beneath their jackets.

With their bodies pressed hard to the ground, was it possible Paul could feel the vibrations of their hearts pounding—thumping in a fast rhythm from inside their chests, down into the ground, spreading out across the cornfield until finally the vibrations might be picked up through Paul's boots, keying him in to their exact location.

That's when they saw it happen.

That's when Paul stepped toward them.

They had seconds to decide if they should remain easy targets, or leap to their feet and run. At least one of them might make it to safety.

Drew watched as Bruce drew his legs up beneath him, still attempting to remain as low as possible to the ground, while putting himself into a position to spring upwards and run.

He imitated the movements, ever so slowly, ever so quietly.

As Drew brought his second leg up under his body, he lost his balance and fell forward. His hand pressed down hard to catch himself and snapped a lower leaf from the base of a dry cornstalk.

Paul turned toward the sound.

They'd been discovered.

No longer concerned with each breath, they gulped the much-needed supply of air, and exhaled quickly. Their uncontrollable rapid breathing, brought about by their fear, was about to betray them.

Which one of them should make a run for it, and which one would be killed instantly, with just one shot at close range, like Rick?

They watched and waited, with trembling legs, ready to spring away as Paul approached.

With his rifle barrel perched against his shoulder, Paul whistled quietly as he walked.

The hunters continued to watch.

Soon, the figure of a man, the man who, without the least sign of remorse, had shot and killed their companion in cold blood, disappeared into the tall corn.

CHAPTER 20

Bruce and Drew, luckily, were not forced to separate. They were still alive, at least for a while. Paul seemed to have looked right at them and then turned and walked away.

Not planning to shoot birds, but rather flush them out into the open for Rick, they had agreed it might be easier to transverse the cornrows unarmed—an oversight they regretted. Unfortunately, a madman and several rows of corn separated them from their shotguns on the backseat of the Escalade.

Paul had taken their keys and locked the doors, but the keypad at the driver's side door still offered them the opportunity to arm themselves. The challenge was to travel the short distance without being spotted.

Without the keys they couldn't drive away, and might still be forced to go to battle with Paul, who undoubtedly had more experience with guns than they did.

They sat on the ground, back-to-back, to survey the area.

What's worse, seeing Paul and watching his every move, or not knowing where he is or if he can see them?

They waited in silence.

"What should we do?" Bruce whispered, breaking that silence.

"I'm not sure. Maybe we should try to make our way back to the road," answered Drew.

"I think we should stay together," said Bruce.

Not that they could do anything to protect each other against a man with a rifle—a heartless man with military training. But, somehow staying together offered a thin strand of comfort.

They began their slow approach toward the road.

One wrong move, one hasty step into the rows, would cause the dried leaves to release a sound pinpointing their location. Fear had quickly sobered them, reducing the courage that Jack Daniels had provided earlier.

"Wait," said Bruce.

"What?"

Cornstalked

"He's probably expecting us to head back to the road. I think he's planning to ambush us there."

They stopped to discuss their options.

"You might be right," said Drew. "Maybe one of us should stay here and the other should go for help."

"That sounds like a stupid plan. How do we decide which one of us is going to be a sacrifice for the other? Besides, if he kills one of us at the road, what's to stop him from coming back into the corn to finish off the other one?"

Drew screwed up the left side of his mouth as he rethought his idea.

"You're right. We're better off staying together.

Bruce fidgeted then said, "I've gotta take a whiz."

"Me, too," Drew moaned. "Too much booze. I feel like my bladder's gonna burst."

"Yeah, I don't think I can hold it much longer," said Bruce.

"I think we're gonna have to. What if he hears us?" said Drew.

"I wondered about that. Hell, he seems to be part cougar, he'd probably smell it."

Drew said, "Let's not take a chance, at least not now."

Bruce zipped up his partially unzipped jeans.

"I heard dying from a burst bladder is a painful way to go," said Bruce.

"Oh, shut up," said Drew. "If you have to go that bad then just take your chances. I'm going to keep moving."

"Which way should we go?" asked Bruce.

"Well, we don't want to go back to the road, and we don't want to go in the direction we saw him walking, so let's go that way."

Drew pointed toward the south.

They had parked the Escalade on a north/south road headed south. They entered the cornfield going east and Paul had walked east, moving toward the middle then turned toward the north, searching for them.

"Should we walk in a straight line?" asked Bruce.

"No, that would make it too easy to find us," said Drew. "Let's walk down a row for a little while then cross over a couple rows. You know, sort of zigzag path."

The rows were planted east to west. If they walked west they'd come out on the road like Paul expected them to do. If they walked north they might bump into him. So they agreed with the plan to work their way to the east but staggering to the south as they did so. If it worked, they'd pop out on the east end of the cornfield, all the while putting distance between them, knowing Paul had turned toward the north.

Once they made it to the road that bordered the cornfield to the east, they could find a house or some other hunter to help them.

Cornstalked

"I'm sure this is a really stupid question," said Bruce, "but where's your cell phone?"

"I think I left it in the Escalade," he responded while he frantically searched his pockets. "Where's yours?"

"I left it in the Escalade so I wouldn't lose it," responded Bruce.

"Wait, wait. I think I found it," said Drew.

Bruce scanned carefully in every direction around them, while Drew pulled the only hope for their rescue from his pocket.

A smile of relief crossed Drew's face.

As they stood deep inside of a cornfield, on a cold, snowy day in Perkins County, Nebraska, being stalked by a crazy man, both men managed to smile and hope.

Drew opened his phone. The small screen on the phone failed to light up.

"Wait, it's probably shut off," said Drew.

He pressed and held the power button.

"Stop," said Bruce. He placed his hand over Drew's. "I hear something."

The two men dropped to the ground again, their hearts pounding in their ears.

Had Drew continued to press the button for one second longer, the song, signaling the phone turning on, would have alerted Paul.

They held their breath as they waited and listened.

Patricia Bremmer

A male, ring-necked pheasant darted along the side of them as it made its way through the corn.

The men froze in place. If that bird saw them, it would immediately take flight and cackle as it flew, drawing all of Paul's attention in their direction.

Earlier in the day, they desperately wanted to flush out and take the lives of dozens of pheasants. This wild bird of the plains, so close to them, could cost them their lives—how ironic.

CHAPTER 21

Their adrenaline raced. Sweat beaded on their foreheads. Frightened and full of liquor, they were reminded of the need to relieve themselves, but how could they, when they agreed the sound of them urinating could be deadly.

They crouched down close to the ground, blood rushing through their veins and pounding in their ears. They watched as the once hunted bird held their fate. Slowly, he crept through the leaves, his feet leaving the three-toed pattern in the snow—the track that caused hunter's adrenaline to rise for other reasons. His bright red head was held low as he made his way further and further away from the two men who succeeded in making themselves invisible to the bird. Less than an hour ago, they were the hunters and he was their prey, now they are the prey being hunted by one with ten times their skill.

Finally, after what seemed an eternity, the bird disappeared into the corn without taking flight. The men gasped for air and felt their pulse ease back to normal.

Drew and Bruce scanned the area for Paul then turned their attention back to the cell phone.

Drew reached into his pocket to retrieve the phone for a second time. He had slipped it into his pocket as a precaution if the pheasant did take flight, causing them to run. Keeping it in his hand while they worked their way through the cornstalks might have increased his chances of losing it. Besides, he needed his hands to brush the sharp stalks and leaves away from his face as he ran through them.

It was gone. The cell phone was missing.

He checked another pocket—no phone.

Bruce studied the panic on Drew's face, and urged him with his eyes to keep looking.

Drew, after searching every pocket of his hunting jacket, dropped to his knees to check the snow. That's when he caught a glimpse of the shiny blue phone. With gloved hands, he had misjudged his pocket while his eyes were glued to the pheasant, and accidentally dropped it onto the ground when he missed his pocket entirely, and the snow had filled in over it, concealing all but a sliver of the blue cover.

Cornstalked

He picked it up and brushed it off.

Bruce turned in a complete circle looking for Paul. They held their breath and listened. The silence that surrounded them told them they were alone for the moment.

Drew unzipped his jacket and pressed the phone close to his chest as he pressed the power button. He hoped between his chest and the heavy jacket that the music would be muffled enough to allow them to remain hidden.

He heard the weak melody finish then took the phone out to dial 911. His battery light started to flash. He listened carefully as the phone rang at the 911 operator's desk.

Then he heard the man's voice, "911, what's your emergency?"

"We need help," whispered Drew.

"I'm sorry, I can't hear you. Can you speak up?"

"We need help," Drew continued.

"Is this a medical emergency? Is someone hurt?"

"Yes, my friend's been shot and we need help."

There was no response.

Drew pulled the phone away from his ear and found the light had gone out. He pressed the power button again, but the weak battery had stopped before he could finish his entire distress message.

"Damn," he said. "It's dead."

"Are you sure?" asked Bruce. "Here, let me try."

He snatched the phone away from Drew and pressed the power button.

Suddenly, Bruce felt totally defenseless. No one knew where he was. No one could protect him from the deadly violence. An ill feeling grew inside him, starting low in his gut. An aching, fluttering movement eased its way up his body. His heart rate increased another notch, as if that was even possible, his breathing turned to a shallow pant, and his throat tightened as he held back the urge to cry out for help. The sensation took over his body until, finally, he had to vomit from the fear.

Bruce had never experienced that kind of fear, the kind caused by someone controlling him, someone he couldn't escape from, someone who seemed to enjoy that high level of control.

No longer able to physically manage the sensation, he dropped to his knees and vomited. Having not eaten all day, there was nothing but a few bites of jerky mixed with stomach fluids. He gagged and retched until he could bring up nothing more.

Not once did he draw a connection to how he had made Kimberly feel on the days he chose to beat her. How often had he heard her vomit before an anticipated attack?

A controller can never empathize with his victim, but chooses to make excuses, justifying the motives for punishment by placing the blame onto the victim in response to something she did or did not do to deserve the abuse.

But being stalked by Paul was different. Bruce felt he had done nothing to deserve the punishment Paul was dishing out. After all, if Paul had just allowed them to hunt his trees, the outcome would have been entirely different.

Bruce was totally unaware of Kimberly feeling ill at that exact moment. Ill from the fear that the important phone call concerning Bruce's promotion might not happen.

CHAPTER 22

Drew and Bruce knew they must perfect each detail of their escape plan—a way to outwit their predator. The most obvious option would be to sacrifice one of them by distracting Paul while the other ran as fast as he could, and didn't stop until he found someone on the road to help. One more life would be lost, but their assailant would be brought to justice. That had to be worth something. Obvious or not, neither one wanted to become the martyr for their cause, so that subject was closed, never to be mentioned again.

"What should we do?" whispered Drew, hoping Bruce, who always had an answer for everything, would have one now.

"Shhh," said Bruce.

Cornstalked

The crunching sound of dried cornstalks warned them as Paul drew nearer.

"I can't believe we left our guns behind," whispered Drew.

Paul was close enough they could hear his quiet whistle.

"We'd better get moving," whispered Bruce.

Slowly, the two men eased away from the sound of the footsteps.

Paul, a master hunter, paused to watch and wait.

The two men tried to walk while squatting down, but they made no progress, falling over onto the ground with each step. With no other choice but to increase their speed and distance, they rose up slightly and moved forward.

Paul caught a glimpse of their orange hats. "Morons," he mumbled.

He watched for a few seconds as the two bright orange heads bobbed up and down across the rows.

"They couldn't survive one day at war," he spoke quietly, as if he were speaking to another soldier on patrol with him. Had his mind slipped back to "kill or be killed" from his tour of duty? Was he aware these men were not enemy soldiers? Or were they simply disposable lives? Did he feel justified in being both judge and jury by taking the future of their lives into his own hands? Or was he merely entertaining himself for the day?

He raised his rifle and sighted them in, first one and then the other. He knew, from that distance, he could easily drop them both with just two shots. What was he waiting for?

"I don't think he saw us," said Drew.

Excitement mounted as they sneaked through the corn further and further from their assailant. Bruce turned back to see if Paul was following. He couldn't see him.

"What the hell? Is he blind or are we just lucky?" asked Bruce.

"Shhh," said Drew. "He might be closer than we think."

They stopped to listen.

Nothing, not a sound, except for the slight rustling of cornstalk leaves from the increasing breeze.

"I think we can take a break," said Bruce.

No food, fear, and exhaustion intensified by the situation, aided in the slightly overweight men requiring more rest stops than a more fit individual, like Paul.

"Which direction are we going?" asked Drew.

"I'm not sure. The sun's gone behind the clouds. I've lost my sense of direction. I think we're still heading southeast."

"He found us pretty fast considering he went off to the north and we kept moving," said Drew.

"That's what I thought," replied Bruce.

Cornstalked

"He must be tracking us like animals. God knows we've been leaving an easy trail to follow."

They looked down at the snow. Their footprints left bold marks between the rows. A child could follow them.

"We should cover our tracks," said Drew.

"Yeah, but how?"

"I don't know," said Drew.

He searched the ground, but an answer failed to come to mind. "We'd better start moving again. I can't see him and that makes me nervous," said Drew.

"Okay. But let's try to cross the rows instead of walking between them. It'll make tracking us more difficult. Maybe it's a good thing it clouded over," said Bruce.

Drew stood up again and tried to ease his thick-coated body through the tightly planted rows of corn without creating movement or sound.

Bruce followed his lead.

It was impossible not to make the tall stalks bend and sway with every brush of their coats.

Paul watched from his post, never moving. No need to. He learned, a long time ago, as a child, to let the prey expose its path. That lesson was re-enforced by his military training.

He had trained as a sniper. Having grown up as many country kids do, he learned to handle a rifle at an early age, first to shoot predators to protect chickens and other livestock, then to help feed the family by bringing home game. Handling a rifle was second nature to Paul.

He aced all the target practices during his military training. He earned extra money on the side by betting he could hit a selected target at an agreed upon distance. His sergeant took note of his keen abilities.

After several weeks of training, the soldiers were lined up for yet another practice session.

"Today men," began his sergeant. "We'll watch and score. We'll then pick the cream of the crop from among you. Give it your all today. Make it count."

One young soldier standing in front of Paul raised his hand.

"Yes?"

"What will we be selected for?" asked the naïve, young man.

"The best of you will be given the honor of becoming a sniper. Again, we only want the cream of the crop."

The target practice began.

Paul missed every target.

His sergeant stood next to him while he fired his rifle.

"Having an off day?" he asked.

"No sir, just a regular day. Can't hit the broad side of a barn."

Cornstalked

"Funny how well you shoot when money's on the table."

"It is funny, isn't it, sir."

Both men knew exactly what was happening. Paul had no intention of joining the ranks of sniper. He was too aware that the snipers would be positioned alone, in high places like a church steeple, and would also be the first ones to be taken out by the enemy. The key was to use the sniper to drop as many men as possible before his location became apparent.

Paul, a wise country lad, knew how to save his own skin. He suddenly lost his ability to hit targets and was disqualified early during the competition.

He would've most likely been one of the most talented snipers ever to join the army. His ability as a marksman continued to increase as he matured.

With his rifle perched against the front of his shoulder, his calm, blue eye looked down the barrel to the tip as he lined up his target. Without the slightest movement or sway, he drew in a breath and eased his finger onto the trigger.

He squeezed.

CHAPTER 23

The top of a cornstalk bent in two from the hit by the .22 caliber bullet.

Terrified, the two men squatted down and forced their eyes to penetrate the rows of corn in search of Paul. Without knowing from which direction the shot had come, they didn't know which direction to run.

They froze.

"Can you tell where that came from?" asked Bruce.

"No."

"Must've been from the last place we saw him," said Bruce.

"Yeah, unless he circled around us," Drew pointed out.

"How far do you think the bullet traveled?"

Cornstalked

"How the hell should I know, you're the expert here."

"If we can't see him, how can he see us?" asked Bruce.

"I don't know. It's like he's invisible or something," said Drew.

"That's it," said Bruce. "His clothes, he's dressed in a light brown jacket with a tan cap, making him invisible against the cornstalks."

"How can you remember that?" asked Drew.

"I have the image of him dragging Rick into the corn burned into my mind. I'll never be able to let that one go."

"Our hats," said Drew.

"What about them?"

He looked at Drew's head and the bright orange stocking cap that served its purpose far too well. A beacon in the corn to stop an accidental shooting by another hunter, gave Paul a definite advantage.

Immediately, they removed their hats and stuffed them into their pockets.

"Okay, now that we fixed that stupid ass problem, which way should we go?" asked Bruce.

"I wish we could see the sun. I have no idea which direction we're going. Let's continue straight ahead while we angle to the right, and hope to God he's still behind us and we're not walking toward him," said Drew.

Patricia Bremmer

Slowly, they crawled on their hands and knees; rough ground beneath the snow sliced their wrists, highlighting their path with red droplets on the snow. Broken cornstalks cut the exposed flesh on their faces. They brushed the red snow, smearing the blood into a bright shade of pink.

It didn't matter. Even without the blood or the indentations and drag marks left behind, Paul could easily track them.

They crawled for what seemed like a mile, although it had been less than a quarter of the distance. The fear and anxiety of being lost in a cornfield always causes a panicked person to misgauge directions and distance.

Surely, they'd soon come to the end of a row and find a road, or a house, or someone to save them from the barbarian who had killed their friend.

That might have been possible had they followed just one row to the end, but they continued to cross rows, failing to walk in a straight line. They weaved back and forth, increasing their time but not shortening their distance.

They stopped to rest.

CHAPTER 24

Paul, zeroing in on their location, passed them several rows over and stood ahead of them while they looked back toward the direction they had come.

Crawling along only seemed to slow them down and make it easier for Paul, who stood tall and slender, to slither through the corn like an upright snake, all the while remaining invisible to his prey.

"We need to keep going," said Drew. "We can't keep stopping to rest like this."

Bruce, unnerved by everything around him, still found the balls to become defensive with Drew for daring to give him orders.

"I'll say when we move and when we rest," said Bruce in an attempt to regain his control.

"Fine, we'll stay here like a pair of sitting ducks. Hell, maybe when he walks right up to us, we'll sit around and have a nice chat about our families," said Drew.

Bruce looked at his watch.

"You're not still worried about that damned phone call, are you?" asked Drew.

"My future depends on it," said Bruce.

"I thought you said you definitely had the job," answered Drew angrily.

"I do, I'm sure I do. I'm just hoping Kimberly doesn't miss the call."

"Your future depends on us getting out of here, to hell with the phone call. That job's not going to do you much good if you're dead. You know, if it wasn't for you and that stupid promotion we wouldn't be in this situation. I'd be home having a nice weekend snowed in with Gina," said Drew.

"You can't blame me for this. How was I supposed to know there's lunatics running around Perkins County with guns?"

"Don't forget," said Drew. "It was you who decided to go against this guy's warning not to hunt on his property. If we would've just driven to the next field we wouldn't be here running for our lives."

"Okay, okay. I made a few stupid judgment calls. There, does that make you feel better. Do you feel superior now?"

Cornstalked

Drew stood up.

"What are you doing?" asked Bruce.

"I'm moving on and I'm not stopping until I get out of this god forsaken maze. I don't give a damn whether you stay or leave."

Bruce struggled to his feet, losing his balance on the slippery ridge where the cornstalks protrude from the ground. He twisted his ankle as his foot slid at an angle into the furrow. Without thinking, he reached out for the nearest cornstalk to break his fall.

A shot rang out, and, once again, a cornstalk above their heads broke and fell to the ground. The two men scattered in opposite directions, playing into Paul's plan.

His intention all along was to separate them. He could've hit them with his first two shots, but he enjoyed the taunting game, much like a cat with a mouse. He sensed their fear; it hung heavy in the air. The feeling of being stalked and all alone should intensify that terror.

That second shot, so close, caused them to finally empty their full, aching bladders. Strong wind gusts broke the calm in the cornfield. Not knowing whether the rustle of the leaves was from Paul approaching or the wind blowing across the tops of the stalks amplified the panic. Between the gusts, the deadly calm returned. The intermittent bursts of wind, and the absence of the sun, would cause the men to chill in their wet clothes.

Patricia Bremmer

Bruce and Drew having been separated gave at least one of them a chance for survival. Had they separated early on, one of them might possibly have already made it to the road for help and their nightmare would have ended.

Tears flowed down in a steady stream, falling from Bruce's red, chapped cheeks as he struggled to put distance between himself and Paul. Cold, wet, hungry, tired, petrified, and in pain from his twisted ankle, he forced himself to keep moving. The thought crossed his mind to stop and confront Paul. To put an end to the torment quickly sounded like a viable option, but in the end, his desire to survive surpassed his desire to surrender.

CHAPTER 25

Paul knew he planned to kill the hunters. The hunters knew he planned to kill them, and they wondered how much longer their luck would hold out. But this wasn't about luck. The stalking was more about the chase, the exhilaration for a man who lived such a peaceful, non-eventful existence in his small, boringly quiet, rural community.

Drew had changed his course after the last shot was fired. Completely disoriented he wandered aimlessly, hoping to find some clue as to the direction he was traveling.

He tried to remember, when they originally entered the cornfield, which direction the rows were planted.

Could he see down the rows or was he looking across the rows?

What the hunters didn't know was that they were not trapped in just one cornfield but four connected fields. If they had walked a mile in any direction, provided they walked a straight line, they'd find that much sought after county road—their only means of escape.

Paul knew exactly what he was doing. He had spent thousands of hours on a saddled horse in cornfields and pastures, slowly and methodically moving and gathering herds of cattle.

His calm way taught him to expend little energy and to ease his horse around the outside edge of the cattle and move them into a horseshoe pattern, tightening up the sides, as he moved them toward the open end.

Guiding the hunters, he lacked the added benefit of the cattle seeing the horse and rider and wanting to move away from them. Out here he knew that Drew and Bruce couldn't see him, and they wouldn't see him if he could help it. He maintained his edge.

Paul knew it was necessary to take his time, necessary for daylight to fade before he could finish. He pulled from his past experiences as he slowly and methodically tracked Drew. It was easy. He followed the sound of Drew's breathing, his feet crunching the dried vegetation, and when that failed, the pheasants that were flushed up as he approached.

Cornstalked

Occasionally he'd fire another shot to turn Drew in the direction he wanted him to walk. Then he'd go off in search of Bruce to herd him in the same direction, assuming the two hunters would never meet up again with the distance between them being too far, and them growing more and more fatigued as the minutes ticked by.

After another hour had passed, he tired of the chase and moved in for the kill. He had to make a choice at this point as to which one to pursue and which one might think he could possibly slip away. He made his decision. He positioned himself, once again, ahead of his prey. He waited, spotted his victim, took aim and, at the last second, lifted the barrel and shot into the air.

"I'll swear," he murmured.

Just as Paul had raised his rifle to drop one of the unsuspecting hunters, he noticed the other making his way back to join the intended victim.

The sound of the crunching snow after the last gunshot left the two separated hunters on edge, wondering where their assailant might be. Again, if at all possible, the rate of their breathing increased even more. Their hearts pumped harder, sending a rush of blood throughout their chilled bodies.

Beneath the several layers of hunting garb, sweat trickled down their backs. Although it was windy with below freezing temperatures, they felt sickly hot. They were experiencing the feeling that flu and fever bring on—nausea, trembling, cold sweats.

Each knew that the sound he heard, so nearby, was the final sound he would ever hear. Each prepared to feel the piercing of the bullet as it passed through the hunting jacket deep into his chest.

It was over. Paul had finished the hunt and was prepared to move in for the kill.

Drew turned his back to the sound of footsteps in the snow. He preferred not to watch death coming. He waited, trembling and shivering from the fear and cold.

Closer and closer the footsteps pressed hard against the snow, no attempt was made to quiet the impact, to disguise the approach.

Drew wrapped his lower teeth around his upper lip as he sucked it inside his mouth waiting, still waiting. What's taking him so long? Damn it, just shoot.

He could feel the approach. He could see the breath of the man, standing only inches behind him, rise up and spread out. Drew refused to turn to face him. He planned to force the monster to shoot him in the back and not give him the satisfaction of seeing the fear in his eyes and watching his face as death took him.

If Paul was going to kill him, he had to shoot him in the back, like a coward.

Please just get it over with. Drew's thoughts raced. Maybe this time Paul had a knife. Maybe his death wouldn't be as quick and painless as Rick's death. Maybe Paul planned to torture him slowly.

Suddenly, he felt the gloved hand cover his mouth. He waited for the feel of the knife, the cold blade penetrating his body.

Drew, unable to turn around, could do nothing but wait. Each second ticked away more slowly then he'd ever experienced. So this is what a slow death feels like.

His assailant pressed his body close to Drew's back and whispered into his ear.

"Don't scream out. It's me, Bruce. I didn't think I was going to be able to find you."

Drew turned toward Bruce. Tears flowed down his face. He dropped to his knees to sob.

"Come on let's get out of here. He's close by. I saw his tracks. Two can play at this game."

CHAPTER 26

Paul watched as the two men rejoiced in being reunited. He gave them that. He waited and allowed them to move away from him. He had orchestrated his chase to herd his victims closer to the edge of the field where the game had begun.

Although he planned to keep them separated, he still had plenty of time to let them move along before he forced them to part ways once again.

"I found his tracks and I think I found ours," said Bruce. "At least, I saw some blood along the path and the snow was trampled. I don't think he's hurt."

"Could it be Rick?" Drew's voice raced with excitement. "Do you think he was not dead after all, but only unconscious?"

Cornstalked

"I don't know," said Bruce. "I kind of doubt it."

"If it is Rick, he has a gun," said Drew.

Bruce allowed himself the pleasure of hope. Hope that Drew was correct and Rick was actually still alive and looking for them. Hope that Rick would outsmart Paul and take him by surprise, killing him before he killed one of them. Hope that the three of them would walk out alive with a wildly crazy story to tell.

That small shred of hope was all they needed for the moment to keep them going.

Drew noticed Bruce dragging his right leg in the snow.

"Are you shot?" he asked.

"No. I think I might have sprained my ankle," said Bruce.

"Can you put weight on it?" asked Drew.

"Some," responded Bruce.

"I'll bet it's not sprained, maybe just twisted," said Drew.

"Whatever. It hurts like hell and it's slowing me down. Let's keep going, unless you want to move on alone?"

"No, I think two sets of eyes are better than one."

"I know what you mean. I don't think we were separated for more than twenty minutes but it seemed like hours," said Bruce.

"Stupid, isn't it?" said Drew as they trudged along.

"What's that?"

"Neither one of us has a gun, or any means to protect each other, but we still feel safer together. This is one scary place when you're alone."

"It's just as scary when we're together. Now shut up and keep moving. I don't want him to hear us," said Bruce, taking the leadership position once again.

"How far do you think he can see with dusk coming on?" asked Drew.

"Far enough. Now I mean it, shut up or you're on your own," said Bruce.

In silence, they followed their trail back toward the center of the cornfield. From there they might be able to find their way out to the road.

CHAPTER 27

In one short afternoon lost in a cornfield, short by the clock but an eternity for the hunters, they had learned to pace themselves. They'd walk a few steps and stop. That way when they moved the cornstalks, alerting Paul to their location, by the time he'd turn to look, the leaves would be still again.

They learned the art of survival from watching the pheasants they encountered along the way. If the pheasants had the chance to watch the hunters approach, and if the men stopped for a few seconds then moved on, the birds would have the opportunity to weave their way through the stalks for cover without feeling threatened. Generations of pheasants instinctively knew that remaining on the ground, rather than flying up and giving away their location, would save their lives.

In their short time striving for survival, they had learned much about eluding their assailant. But, how much more does Paul know having spent his entire life studying the movement of animals in their natural habitat?

Bruce had a new appreciation for hunting and what it meant to be the hunted. But, he thought, at least the birds or deer he hunted had no idea they were being stalked. They didn't experience the intense fear that he and Drew shared.

"I have to ask you something," whispered Bruce when they stopped to take another break.

They hoped with each break it confused Paul. There would be no movement, no sound, and no sightings. If they were lucky, he'd turn back rather than moving forward to follow them.

"What?" asked Drew.

"Why didn't you run when you heard me coming back there? You *did* hear me coming, didn't you?"

"Oh yeah, I heard you alright. But I thought you were him. I thought I had nowhere to run. I guess you could say I was giving up. I just wanted him to put me out of my misery as quickly as possible," said Drew.

"I felt that way, too. When I was alone, dragging my foot, I had a moment when I just wanted it to end. I even thought about doing it myself so he wouldn't have the satisfaction."

"What stopped you?" asked Drew.

"I can't let him win without a fight."

"How do you fight someone like him?"

"I had a little time to think about that while I was alone. What do you think about us turning the tables and tracking him?"

Drew smirked, "And then what, Rambo, wrestle him to the ground and take away his rifle? What chance do we have unarmed?"

"That's just it, we're not unarmed," said Bruce. "I have my hunting knife and you have yours."

"I smell a really foul plan here," said Drew.

"Fine, let's just keep walking and let him pluck us off one after the other. I'm okay with that if you are. Might as well just stand up and wave our arms and yell to him. That could speed things up," said Bruce.

He stood up to walk away.

"Wait, what's your plan?" asked Drew. "It can't hurt to listen to it."

Bruce turned around, scanned the area, watched for movement then sat down.

"I thought maybe one of us could lie down on the ground and pretend to be dead and when he finds the body, he'll probably bend down to check it out and then the other one can jump him from behind with a knife."

"It's remotely possible that that might work, but which one of us is going to play dead? And, what's to stop him from putting a bullet or two into the body to be sure it's dead before he approaches it?" asked Drew.

"It's a chance I'm willing to take," said Bruce. "We can't let him win."

"This isn't about winning or losing. This is about staying alive," said Drew.

"What do you say? Are you game?" asked Bruce.

"Please use a different choice of words," said Drew. "Are you going to play dead? Cause, I'm not going to take that chance."

"I'm bigger than you are and more experienced with a knife," Bruce pointed out.

"I take it that means your answer is no?" said Drew.

Bruce had no intentions of putting his own life on the line beyond the danger he was currently in, but also had no qualms about jeopardizing the life of his companion.

"You're right," said Bruce. "It's a stupid idea."

CHAPTER 28

"We should keep moving," said Drew.

The heavy, gray clouds overhead had thickened. Various shades of gray blocked even the tiniest hint of sun from coming through, as it was about to set. Areas of the clouds were pale, dismal, sad colors, while the rest were an angry, threatening, darker shade. To interpret the meaning of the clouds you might say there was more darkness looming ahead for the hunters without a sign of hope.

Both men were drained of all energy. Fatigue from the cold, the fear, and stumbling around through the never-ending maze of corn left them with the feeling of defeat. Even Bruce seemed to lose his edge, his desire to be in control. That feeling of hope they had found earlier had faded into despair.

The temperature made a steady decline after the sun disappeared behind the clouds. The breeze turned into a brisk wind. Their lungs ached from breathing in the frigid air. The skin on their faces grew more chapped and red. Their lips were split and bleeding from the rapid breathing through their open mouths.

Wet clothes clung to their bodies and sucked the warmth from their skin. Hypothermia was moving in. The desire to stop and curl up into a ball to conserve energy was strong. But, staying in one spot for too long increased the chances that Paul would find them.

If he did find them, their pain and suffering would end quickly. One bullet for each of them and the cold would fade away, as would the terror.

"I'm getting so cold," said Drew as his teeth chattered ever so slightly when he spoke.

"I know. Me, too," said Bruce.

"Do you think he'll leave when it gets dark?" asked Drew.

"I hadn't thought of that, but you're right. He probably will. He might be an animal, but I'll bet he can't see in the dark like one," said Bruce.

"Maybe if we can avoid him long enough, we can find our way out after darkness sets in," said Drew hopefully.

Cornstalked

"I don't think he'll let that happen," said Bruce.

"Why?"

"Because we saw what he did to Rick. We're eye witnesses," said Bruce.

"Yeah, but we don't know if Rick is really dead. Don't forget the blood we saw. It could be Rick out looking for us, and he has a gun. This isn't over yet," said Drew with a new burst of desire to survive.

"I have another idea," said Bruce.

"What is it?"

"The first one wasn't that bad, but it had a potentially fatal flaw for one of us. But what if we only let him think he's stumbled across one of us collapsed in the corn. Then we ambush him from behind with the knives."

"I don't see where you're going with your thinking," said Drew.

"What if we make a body that can take our place?" said Bruce.

"I don't follow."

"We can use one of our coats and bib overalls to make it look like one of us," said Bruce.

"I get it. We can fill it with corn leaves to fluff it up. Laying face down in the snow he won't know until he gets right up to it that it's not one of us. Then if he chooses to shoot it before approaching, we'll be safe. He's bound to squat down to check it and that's when we stab him."

"Yeah, but one of us is going to freeze without the extra clothes," said Drew.

"I'm willing to give up a layer to live," said Bruce.

"Okay then. Let's get started," said Drew.

Slowly Bruce removed his jacket, then his bibbed overalls.

Drew had already begun stripping leaves from the cornstalks. Using his knife, he quickly learned how to hold the stalk still and slice the leaves creating a minimum amount of movement and nearly no sound.

Together, the two men stuffed the crisp golden leaves into the jacket and pants.

"We can use my boots," offered Drew.

Bruce rolled and fashioned snow to form a head to fill the jacket's hood, raising it up from the ground as if a real head was inside.

They attached Drew's boots then stood back to look at their creation.

"I don't know," said Drew. "Something doesn't look right."

They studied it a little longer.

"I think it's the way he's laying," said Bruce. "He looks too stiff, too fake."

They manipulated their corn leaf scarecrow into a series of different poses until they finally arrived at one that looked like a real man had collapsed from exhaustion.

Cornstalked

"That'll work," said Bruce, bouncing up and down, trying to stay warm.

"Here, you take my coat," said Drew.

"Then you'll get cold," said Bruce.

"We'll take turns with it," said Drew. "We'll each wear it for ten or fifteen minutes."

"Good idea," said Bruce.

"What do we do next?" asked Drew.

"We make some noise now. Rustle the corn really loud. Draw his attention to this spot. Then we'll wait."

"But we won't know which direction he's coming from," Drew pointed out.

"That's just the risk we're going to have to take. We have a seventy-five percent chance he's not going to come up behind us. We have to take that chance," said Bruce.

They examined their lure one last time then Bruce shook the cornstalks near the body several times.

Then from out of nowhere came another shot. It zoomed past their heads.

"Could you tell which direction that came from?" asked Drew.

"I think it came from over there," said Bruce as he pointed to his left.

"Okay, then we need to hide. He'll be coming from that direction."

The two men parted ways. Each took his post on opposite sides of where the body lay. That way when Paul came to check out the area, he wouldn't stumble onto both of them at once. And hopefully, he'd not find either of them, but would spot the body laying face down in the snow first.

They waited in silence.

CHAPTER 29

Bruce checked his watch. It was 3:30. Soon it would be too dark to see anything. He looked up at the clouds. They were miraculously thinning. In the west he saw the slightest sliver of orange and pink. The sun was descending below the horizon. The light of day might be fading, but his excitement over learning their location intensified.

He wondered if Drew had noticed.

They waited.

Where is he? Surely Paul would want to make his way toward the spot he had sent his last bullet zooming past.

Anxiously, Bruce checked again—3:45.

He pulled his coat, actually Drew's coat, closer to his bare neck. His hood was on the jacket he forfeited to the fake body. His fingers gripped his hunting knife tightly. So tightly that he could barely feel them. First, numbing from the cold and then his tight grip slowed the blood from flowing into his fingertips.

He was uncertain how his cold hands would work when he needed to use them. Envisioning the blade slicing deeply into the front of Paul's throat while Drew pierced his cold heart, increased his pulse, and sent a burst of warmth throughout his chilled body.

He rubbed his hands together then tried blowing hot air inside his gloves, hoping to feel his fingers again.

And he waited.

Drew, squatting directly across from Bruce, no more than six feet from the furrow containing their decoy, strained to catch a glimpse of Bruce.

Somehow, he still didn't have full trust in him. He wouldn't be the least bit surprised if Bruce changed his mind and disappeared into the corn, leaving Drew and the fake body behind. Drew, without warm clothes, would have no choice but to undress the dummy in an attempt to prevent his body from surrendering to frostbite.

He rubbed his arms vigorously, attempting to keep the blood flowing. His body began to shiver uncontrollably. He moved his knife from one hand to the other. Finally, he could no longer feel his feet, wearing nothing but two layers of socks failed to prevent the icy cold snow from penetrating. The ache went deep into his bones. Sitting down had to be the only way to save his toes.

Rearranging himself, he sat crossed-legged in a half lotus yoga pose hoping his feet might absorb some of his rapidly leaving body heat. He questioned his ability to stand and walk or run, if necessary, on numb feet.

Actually, he questioned the entire plan. He felt hopeless and helpless in the frigid conditions.

Drew's eyes scanned the area, straining to see, as the light faded. That's when he caught a fleeting glimpse of the sun—nothing more than the same orange and pink streak that had caught Bruce's attention.

He smiled to himself. He knew that to his right he could find the road. He had long since given up the idea of trying to move east, not knowing how much further it would be to a road.

All he had to do was ease his way down the row where he sat waiting and that row would take him to a definite exit from the cornfield. He wasn't sure how far north or south of the Escalade he would pop out, but the road meant survival.

He decided then and there, no matter what Bruce said, he would no longer cross rows. He chose a sure thing, a straightforward and speedy exit.

Should he start now and leave Bruce to fend for himself? Could Bruce finish Paul by himself? What about Rick? Why hadn't they spotted him or heard a confrontation between he and Paul?

As Drew shifted his position again, he rubbed his cold feet. He knew he needed his boots to make it to the road. He was tempted to take them back and give up this potentially futile plan in favor of escape.

His thoughts raced with the concept of freedom. Soon it overpowered his desire to stop Paul. He just wanted to be released from the purgatory of the cornfield.

Snap. The sound of a cornstalk brought him back to the immediate problem at hand.

Bruce heard it, too.

They both turned to the east.

Crunch. The sound of walking on the stiff snow alerted them that someone or something was coming.

Bruce pulled in his body as tightly as possible, attempting to become invisible.

Drew slowly unfolded his legs, positioning his feet beneath his body, hoping he'd be able to stand on numb feet at a moment's notice.

They waited and listened.

Silence. Nothing but silence.

It started again. The cornstalks cracked and bent forward as the distance between them and their assailant diminished.

Cornstalked

Drew shifted onto his feet to be certain they worked. He couldn't feel them but they supported his weight and followed the lead of his legs—the best he could hope for.

Bruce drew in a deep breath and held it. His knife raised and ready to rush forward.

Closer and closer, the sound grew louder. They could see the cornstalks moving.

Their hearts pounded so hard in their chests they were certain Paul would be able to hear them. The pumping grew deafening.

With less than three feet to the body lying on the ground, the intruder stepped forward, revealing himself.

A large buck deer moved into view, his full rack of antlers causing the cornstalks to bend and break as he approached the dummy lying on the ground. He stopped, sniffed the air, and bounded away.

CHAPTER 30

Each man released a sigh. Their breathing slowed as it returned to normal, at least, normal for the situation that entangled them.

Being slightly overweight, and lacking toned bodies, their blood pressure was already slightly elevated on any given day. It's amazing, that under the stress they'd experienced during the stalking, that a heart attack hadn't managed to put an end to at least one of them during their attempted flight.

Drew wanted to draw Bruce's attention to the time. He needed the warmth of his coat. It had already been twenty minutes and they had agreed upon sharing the coat every fifteen or twenty minutes.

Cornstalked

Shivering uncontrollably, Drew scanned the long rows of corn where the fake body lay. He stepped into the open space between the rows, attempting to cross over to join Bruce. His feet failed him and he fell to the ground.

Scrambling to his feet caused a loud rustling of the cornstalks.

Finally, he managed to stand on the nearly frozen pegs at the end of his legs. Painfully, he took steps toward Bruce before falling again.

Bruce stood back and watched, not attempting to assist Drew.

He knew that the commotion Drew had caused by stumbling and disturbing the solitude of the corn would draw Paul's attention and allow their plan to work. If Drew's life needed to be sacrificed in the process, so be it. After all, it was Drew's choice to step out of his hiding spot and move into view.

"Bruce," whispered Drew.

Bruce remained still.

"Bruce. Are you there?" asked Drew. "I need my coat."

The silence caused Drew to re-think his previous thought that Bruce might leave him alone to either freeze to death or be killed.

Anger mounted in Drew at the realization of what Bruce had done. That anger caused his pulse to quicken and he felt the hot rush of blood throughout his entire body. That anger gave him the much-needed ability to keep moving without giving his nearly frozen feet much thought.

He crossed two more rows and, to his surprise, he found Bruce squatting ahead of him.

"Why didn't you answer me, you son of a bitch?" asked Drew.

"I didn't want to give up my location. You found me, so that's all that matters," said Bruce.

"I want my coat back," insisted Drew.

"It hasn't been twenty minutes yet," said Bruce.

"Give me my coat or I'll slit your throat," said Drew.

His cold hands raised his knife to strike out at Bruce.

Would Paul need to finish them off or would they do it themselves, given enough time? The desire to survive has a way of turning people against each other in a way that would never materialize under normal circumstances.

There have been dozens of true stories written about the need to survive after being stranded in the cold with no food or way to generate heat. Some stories have come from being lost in blizzards or plane crashes, or the reverse with high heat and being lost in deserts. How far would a man go to survive? That answer is far. Cannibalism to survive is not uncommon.

Would these two hunters, co-workers but not friends, fight to the death over a coat and boots? Why not? That instinct to survive will always supersede social ethics.

"Hey man, what the hell are you doing?" said Bruce. "Here. Take your damn coat. I don't know what's gotten into you, get a grip."

Bruce, when faced with a confrontation against another man, backed down. He only felt powerful against a woman—a woman, like Kimberly, who made no attempt to fight back or defend herself in any way.

Bruce raised himself from his squatting position and took a step back away from Drew. He positioned himself out of range of Drew's knife. He unbuttoned the coat and squirmed his arms from the sleeves, all the while; he kept his eyes focused on the jagged blade pointed directly at him.

Drew stood in front of Bruce like a mugger on the street. He watched Bruce's every move while he intermittently looked up and down the rows and listened for Paul's approach.

Bruce handed the coat to Drew, who stepped back away from Bruce as he slipped his arms into the sleeves. Instantly, he felt the warmth from the coat penetrate the first layer of his skin, warming the outside but driving the cold sensation deeper into his body.

He waved the knife at Bruce, "The boots, too."

"What?" said Bruce. "I'll freeze without a coat or boots."

"I know the feeling," said Drew. "The boots. Don't make me kill you for them."

"You're just as mad as that asshole hunting us," said Bruce.

"Maybe so, but the way I see it, you're the one who got us into this mess and I'm not willing to die to save your sorry ass. You had no intention of sharing the coat or boots with me. You sealed your own fate when you refused to answer me. You were hoping I'd be the one to die first. Well, my friend, that's not the way it's going to be."

Bruce turned to look in every direction before he sat down to remove the boots. He slowly unlaced them.

"Hurry up," said Drew, wielding the knife.

"I can't. I can't feel my hands. I'm trying," said Bruce.

Bruce removed one boot and handed it to Drew.

Drew tried to slip his foot into the boot, but with no feeling left in his feet he couldn't properly guide it. He folded his legs and dropped to the ground. He put the knife between his teeth as he twisted and turned the boot, forcing his foot inside.

Bruce handed the second boot to Drew.

Drew watched Bruce then said, "Both hands in the air. I don't want to see you go for your knife."

"What? You've got to be kidding," said Bruce.

Cornstalked

"Do what I say," said Drew, who had removed the knife from his teeth allowing him the ability to rush forward and stab deep into Bruce's gut.

Bruce could've probably easily overtaken the cold and shivering Drew, but he lacked the courage to make the attempt. Instead, he obediently raised his arms, showing his hands while he waited for Drew to lace up the boots.

"Now what?" asked Bruce.

He had relinquished his role as leader and turned to Drew for instructions.

"I'm going to stay here. You cross over to where I was and we'll follow through as planned," said Drew.

"How do I know I can trust you? How do I know you won't just leave me here?"

"I guess you'll never know for sure, now will you?" said Drew.

CHAPTER 31

Bruce made his way between two rows as he headed toward the spot where Drew had been. He stopped and listened.

He turned quickly, expecting to see Drew behind him with his knife poised to attack. He strained his eyes to look back from where he had started. He saw Drew, waiting as they had planned.

Swish—the unmistakable sound of someone or something moving through the corn.

Bruce waited and tuned his ears for the sound.

Swish, swish.

Earlier, his heart would've thumped loudly as his pulse quickened, but knowing how much wildlife actually lives in cornfields, he had to wonder if it was just another deer or two. It could be a group of pheasants. They had even spotted raccoon tracks near half-eaten corncobs on the ground.

Earlier, he would have turned and rushed back to Drew for help, but not this time. Drew might choose to ignore his plea.

He took his cues from the pheasants they had watched. He lowered his body, attempting to gain invisibility. He remained motionless, except for his eyes. He moved his eyes without moving his head, surveying as much area as possible.

He focused his ears on the approaching sound. His ears felt as if they were turning to listen, rotating like a radar scanner. He knew that was impossible but the sensation was there. Actually, his mind was switching the focus from one ear to the next, attempting to locate the direction of the sound.

That's when he heard it—that god-awful sound that he'd learned to despise. That all too familiar sound— a whistle, a soft, no particular melody, whistle.

It was Paul. He had finally discovered their location.

Bruce stepped back. He eased his to Drew, without turning, he kept his back toward Drew as he walked in reverse. He refused to turn and face Drew, allowing his eyes to miss Paul's approach.

"He's here," he whispered to Drew.

"Are you sure?"

"Yeah, I can hear that damned whistle."

"What should we do?" whispered Drew.

"Attack. What else can we do?"

The two men spaced themselves approximately five feet apart as they crossed the rows.

Slowly and silently they made their approach.

Each step more deafening than the last, not from the noise they made crossing the crunching snow, but from their hearts beating double time within their chests, forcing the pounding to fill their ears to the point that sounds outside their own bodies were inaudible.

Only two rows of corn separated them from Paul.

They eased their way forward, reducing the distance to one row. One thin veil of cornstalks and leaves hid them from the view of their attacker. They froze in place to watch the approach.

Bruce looked toward Drew.

Drew raised his knife, signaling Bruce to do the same.

They waited.

The sound of the whistle grew louder then suddenly dropped off completely.

The men exchanged glances. They knew what had just happened. They knew that Paul had caught sight of the man lying on the ground. What will he do about it?

Cornstalked

Would he risk alerting them to his location by firing his gun? No reason not to. They're unarmed.

"Well, I'll swear," said Paul. "The lazy fat man couldn't handle it."

As he made his way closer to inspect the body, the two hunters stepped out into the row.

Paul, with the butt of his rifle resting on the ground, squatted down to check for a pulse.

Bruce and Drew jumped toward him, knives raised to attack.

They needed to lunge a mere two feet toward him. Stabbing him while he was squatting down or pushing him forward onto the ground to disarm him were their only two choices. Either way, he was destined to feel the cold metal of their knives as they penetrated his body.

Two against one, they had the upper hand.

Paul, unaware and with his back to them, had no chance.

With a split second left before the knives met his body, Paul pushed off of the butt of his rifle, throwing himself into a military move of drop and roll.

In that tiny fraction of time, this ex-soldier, a man now in his late fifties, experienced the physical flashback of war.

Paul pushed off, rolled, raised his rifle, and dropped Drew as he came toward him.

Paul was momentarily thrown off balance by the weight of Drew's body falling forward onto him. He lost the grip on his rifle as he lay under the body.

Paul had hit his head hard on the ground from the impact. The wind was knocked out of him from the dead man's tackle.

Blinking his eyes and drawing in a breath, Paul pushed the heavy weight of the body from his chest. He scanned the ground for his rifle before standing. He didn't want to take the chance of being upright first and then bending over to pick up his rifle, exposing his back to the enemy.

Once he had his rifle in hand, he jumped to his feet in search of the second hunter.

Bruce was nowhere in sight. He had taken advantage of the time it took Paul to regain his composure to disappear into the corn.

CHAPTER 32

Bruce hobbled along as fast as his twisted ankle allowed. Without boots or a coat it was imperative he make his way to the road as quickly as possible. His survival depended upon it.

"Ouch," he mumbled as his foot caught a broken cornstalk that spanned the distance between two rows.

He fell hard. His hands and face were slammed into the icy snow. He could barely breathe. He tried desperately to pull in air, but he failed to fill his lungs to capacity. Tiny short gasps were all he could muster.

The temperature had dropped another ten degrees down to twenty-five. He needed to get up. He needed to run for the road, but every inch of his body ached from both the cold and the impact of hitting the ground with such force.

Blood trickled onto the snow from a scrape on his forehead, just above his left eye. He had no choice. He had to lie there until he could catch his breath. His body refused to allow him an alternative.

***

Several yards behind Bruce, Paul heaved Drew's body over his shoulder as if he were carrying a bag of grain—a daily chore. His plan to herd the hunters closer to the road to avoid having to carry the bodies any distance was thrown off by their feeble attempt to set him up for an ambush. He had no intentions of killing them so deep into the cornfield.

With rifle in hand, Paul turned to look at the makeshift scarecrow on the ground near his foot. He knew he had to return to this spot to retrieve the scarecrow and the clothes. The blood, the clothes, and the pile of leaves would be evidence that something unnatural had happened to the hunters, who would be presumed missing.

"Damn," he mumbled. "I can't believe you idiots had the brains to attempt something so clever. Guess it just wasn't clever enough though, was it?"

He studied the fake corpse a little longer, trying to decide if he should attempt to drag it along. He opted to leave it behind for the time being. He caught a glimpse of orange peeking out from Drew's coat pocket.

He pulled out the bright orange stocking cap and somehow, while still balancing the dead man's body on his shoulder, managed to place the cap on the top of a cornstalk as a flag to mark the spot for his return.

Paul made his way easily through the corn as he headed for the road. Carrying a dead man who probably weighed nearly two hundred pounds didn't seem to faze him. How could that be? Was it sheer strength, or determination, or both?

The clouds had cleared and the sun had set. The air temperature on a clear night in November drops rapidly. The glow from a full moon in Nebraska skies is bright enough to allow someone to read a book. That evening the night sky exhibited a completely full moon, making Paul's task much easier.

***

Bruce lay still on his stomach, as his lungs inflated with the much- needed air. With each new breath he took, he studied the rise and fall of his chest against the hard ground. He waited to feel the sharp pain indicating that he'd broken a rib.

The only real pain he felt came from his face and hands and, of course, his ankle. He rolled onto his back to be absolutely certain he could breath with no discomfort.

He'd heard of people puncturing a lung when a rib is broken and then the jagged edge presses into it. He wondered which way would be the easiest to die. Would it be less painful to continue to lie there until the cold slowly crept into his body, weakening his senses, making him groggy until he finally dozed off to sleep and slowly froze to death or be shot and bleed out if the bullet didn't kill him instantly?

He pulled himself into a sitting position with his arms wrapped around his bent knees to conserve heat.

Or, how would it feel if he did puncture one lung or both. Would he die more or less slowly? And would it be more painful? Then he thought about dying at Paul's hand the way Drew had just died, quick and easy.

It was over for Drew. No more suffering from the cold, no more fear. Was that so bad? Quickly had to be the best way to die.

The same for Rick, Bruce was certain that Paul had succeeded in killing Rick. He knew that madman wouldn't take the chance that Rick would stumble his way to the road and be discovered. He knew, but he didn't want to let Drew know what he had deduced when they spoke about the possibility of Rick still being alive. Bruce wanted to allow Drew that last bit of hope, even though it was strangely out of character for Bruce.

Hope is how Drew died. He died in motion with the hope that he was about to put an end to Paul's murdering spree. Drew had died feeling that last adrenaline rush, the feeling of no longer being hunted but rather a soon to be victorious hunter. The shot was quick and deadly. Drew didn't have time for his brain to register defeat.

But Bruce was still the hunted. Bruce was destined to feel fear until the last moment. There was no sense of victory in his future. The thought of remaining motionless in the cold sounded more appealing to him as time progressed. All he had to do was surrender to it. Go with it. Let sleep overtake him then he'd be unaware of his last breath.

Bruce had made his decision. He'd lie back down on the ground and wait for sleep to take over his body. His mind was totally blank. Isn't your life supposed to flash before you when death approaches? He forced himself to contemplate his life when the memories didn't begin to come to him on their own.

First, his childhood came to mind—not the perfect childhood by far. His parents did not have a vast amounts of money. He was definitely not the most popular kid in elementary school—not pleasant thoughts. How he hated being teased and tormented as a child.

He fast-forwarded to high school. He had gotten a job in the mailroom of an insurance company. He had saved every nickel and dime he possibly could until he could afford to buy his very own car, a 1973 Plymouth Duster, lime green with white stripes, and a spoiler mounted on the back. It was used and slightly abused, but it was his, free and clear. After he had purchased the car, he used his extra money to buy clothes—lots and lots of clothes. He paid to have his hair styled. Then with a car, clothes, and his makeover, came the girls.

He worked energetically at football practice. He pushed himself steadily in order to get ahead. He hated the other boys on the team who could focus on just the games and practices while he had to work to buy all the luxuries the others received as gifts from their parents.

Then his thoughts turned to Kimberly. He had met her in high school and decided shortly after they started dating that she would be his wife. He didn't give her a choice in the matter. He planned every detail of their life.

He hid his plans under the disguise of surprises. Surprise, they were getting married in the Bahamas, on May 13th. He had already made all the plans so she wouldn't have to stress about them.

Surprise, he booked a hall for a big post-wedding party back in Denver and he had already hired a band. Surprise, he'd decided they were going to watch the Los Angeles Rams play football for their vacation; again, all the plans were made before he ran the idea past her. Surprise, he made plans for her birthday dinner and, of course, his when the date came around.

At first she seemed happy with him taking control and handling all of the details of their life. Then, one day, she suggested she might have some say in their plans. That's when it all started. That's when she forced him to hit her the first time. She wasn't at all the girl he had married. No way was she going to second-guess his decisions. He knew what was best for both of them and she should never question his choices.

As he lie between the rows of corn, his body pressed into the cold snow, he worried about Kimberly.

How could she get along without him? She wasn't capable of taking care of herself. He opened his eyes. What would happen to his home and his belongings? Would she allow another man into her life?

He felt the anger rising in him. The strong desire to survive surfaced, even if it was only to prevent her from making foolish mistakes. No way would he allow another man to share *his* house with *his* wife. He'd rather see her dead. He had to return. He had to beat Paul at his own cruel game and escape the prison bars the cornstalks represented.

The rustling of leaves interrupted his thoughts. He turned his head to watch Paul passing two rows over, carrying Drew on his shoulder.

CHAPTER 33

Bruce slid his body back into a prone position. He held his breath as he heard Paul's footsteps in the snow. Slow and deliberate, his stride didn't falter, and still, the weight of a two hundred pound man draped over his shoulder didn't appear to slow him.

Who is this old guy? Bruce learned more about him as the day progressed. He hated him. He feared him. He respected him. Even though he had killed his two companions, and he knew that he was next, he had to respect the man for his abilities—not the meek, mild, old farmer that Bruce had pegged him to be earlier at their first encounter.

Bruce slowed his breathing while Paul passed by, not wanting the steam from his breath to flag his location.

Cornstalked

He waited and listened. No longer could he hear Paul's footsteps in the snow. That meant if he couldn't hear Paul then Paul couldn't hear him.

Bruce scrambled to his feet and ran as fast as he could, bum ankle and cold couldn't stop him. He had to make it back to the scarecrow. He had a chance at survival if he could take back his coat and Drew's boots. He had made it thus far eluding the hunter, and the full moon illuminated his path.

By his estimation, Paul still had a long way to carry Drew to the road, and then he'd have to backtrack to find Bruce. Bruce had finally learned, over the course of the day, the best way to make the swiftest progress was to stay between two rows, and to not cross over.

Without his heavy coat, he made his way down the furrow more easily without disturbing the cornstalks. No leaves rustled, and he was certain that as long as Paul was walking, the crunching of the snow beneath Paul's feet would cover the sound of Bruce's footsteps.

His chest ached from the cold air that filled his lungs as he ran. He had mastered the pain in his ankle by focusing on his escape. At first, he felt his body warming from the jogging, but as the air bit his face, and burned inside his body, fatigue moved in rapidly.

"I can do this," he whispered to himself. "I can do this. It can't be much further."

He focused on the warmth he would gain from the added clothing. The pain had left his feet completely. Actually, all the feeling had left. Frostbite most likely had set in.

He stopped running momentarily to catch his breath. His chest ached so badly that his body almost refused to take in another breath of the cold air. He bent over and placed his hands on his knees. His sides cramped from the lack of oxygen. While he was bent over the moonlight reflected on the snow, highlighting his path and the blood oozing from both feet caught his attention. He had run over the frozen ground with shards of ice and broken stalks slicing his feet through the double layers of socks.

Bruce didn't care. He had to be close to his destination, the spot where the decoy body filled with cornstalk leaves waited, ready to give up its clothes. He wasn't going to be killed. He was going to make it to the coat and boots and then find his way to the road. He was confident.

He straightened his aching body then continued his run.

He had judged his distance well. He didn't have far to go. Just up ahead, no more than four yards from where he had stopped to rest, he caught a glimpse of the orange stocking cap. Instantly, he realized Paul had used it to mark the spot.

Cornstalked

"Thanks for the help, old man," he whispered as he trudged forward.

He snatched the cap from its perch atop the stalk. Squatting down, he rolled the scarecrow over and unbuttoned the coat. He shook it hard, attempting to remove the scratchy bits of leaf residue from the wool lining. Realizing that it was futile, he slid his arms into the sleeves. He wrapped his arms around his body while rubbing each arm in turn, to speed his circulation and create a barrier of warmth between his skin and the cold coat.

Next, he dropped to the ground and removed the boots whose tops were tucked inside the bib overalls. He forced his feet into the boots then grabbed the coveralls and shook them. He wrapped them around his shoulders, planning to take the time to slip into them once he was further away. He knew Paul planned to return and he wanted to be certain he was well on his way toward the road before Paul made it back for the clothes.

He glanced down at the pile of leaves and debris he had left behind. His first thought was to scatter them in an attempt to confuse Paul. Then he decided it didn't matter, Paul had an uncanny ability to track and would easily discover his futile attempt at disguising the true location. It wasn't worth exerting the extra energy or wasting more of his precious time.

He guessed Paul's return would be by the same furrow—the shortest and fastest way to return to this spot to dispose of evidence.

Bruce planned to move several rows to the north, hoping that he could return to the road at the west edge of the cornfield, allowing Paul to pass right by him with his focus on finding the scarecrow to dismember it.

Bruce counted rows, one, two, three, as he crossed over them. He thought an even dozen rows would make it impossible for Paul to notice him, provided his hunch about Paul's path was correct.

Bruce made good time heading west. He adjusted the camouflage bib overalls that he had draped over his shoulders. His hands felt a lump in one of the pockets. He stopped to investigate.

Tucked inside one of the side pockets, on the outside of the knee, he found two sticks of beef jerky, a package of corn nuts, and an unopened package of chewing gum from his last hunting trip.

He bit off a large chunk of jerky then searched the rest of the pockets. He knew time was on his side and he could afford a few minutes to rest and gain strength and nourishment from the much-needed food.

He found four small heat packs, the kind you snap and chemicals inside heat up to warm hands or feet. He snapped two of the small plastic covered heat packs and stuffed them into his gloves.

Cornstalked

He bit off another large chunk of jerky, wrapped the overalls around his neck then continued walking.

CHAPTER 34

Paul dropped Drew's body on top of his first kill of the day then went in search of Bruce. He expected to find Bruce's body, rather than a walking, living target. Drew and the scarecrow each had a coat and boots, which meant that Bruce had neither, and the dropping temperatures would soon put an end to his sorry life.

Paul's biggest concern was that he might not find his body. But then, would that be all bad? Without a gunshot wound he would have appeared to die from exposure. No way to connect that to Paul. His missing friends would be accused of foul play, stripping him of his coat and boots and sending him on his way. The search would be for the two missing survivors.

Cornstalked

Paul had nothing to worry about, once he gathered the evidence he had left behind. He knew finding the clothes stuffed with corn leaves might prove more puzzling to the authorities than if they happened upon Bruce's frozen body.

If he discovered the body himself, he planned to leave it wherever it lay. If he found Bruce alive and making his way out of the cornfield, well then, he'd have no other recourse but to shoot him and eliminate a witness to the day's events.

Bruce continued west, stopping every few minutes to gnaw off another bite of the jerky. The feeling finally returned to his hands, allowing his fingers to bend more easily. A little food in his stomach stimulated his body and improved its ability to function.

His plan was working as he was making his way, slowly and steadily toward the outer edge of the cornfield. If he had timed it correctly, Paul would be away from the road in search of the dismantled scarecrow and Bruce could flag down a driver, or in the best-case scenario, he would actually stumble upon his Escalade.

He sometimes stored a spare key in the console. With the exterior keypad he could easily get inside. If, by chance, Paul had located and disposed of that extra key, at least Bruce would still have access to the interior and the shotguns. He would no longer be defenseless against Paul. It would be a fair battle with both of them armed, and Bruce felt he would have the element of surprise in his favor.

His mind raced frantically with the thoughts of his inevitable escape. What if Paul not only found the extra key, but also disposed of the shotguns from the backseat? Bruce would be totally at the mercy of a passing vehicle. What would the chances be that someone would be out on such a cold and icy night? He refused to let negative thoughts creep in. He had to remain positive and focused.

Paul headed east at a lively pace. It was getting late and he needed to be home to feed his horses and get a bite to eat for himself. He knew Liz would have dinner ready by six.

Bruce checked his watch—4:30. His trek to the west and his freedom remained steady. Once he warmed up from the walk, his ankle ached again as he forced it to hold his weight while he pressed on.

The gap between the two men, Paul moving east and Bruce moving west, closed with each step.

Paul's wide stride covered more than twice the distance of Bruce's hobbled stride, slowed by the pain from his ankle. But regardless, each was making his own way toward his destination.

No more getting lost for Bruce. He had his goal set straight in his mind. The snack had improved his alertness and his mind acted like a compass with his eyes searching due west.

Cornstalked

Paul, relaxed knowing he didn't have to worry about Bruce any longer, had just one last small task to perform then he could finish his work of the day.

Bruce kept his ears and eyes open waiting, for Paul's return.

Paul, although always aware of his surroundings, had given up the search for Bruce whom he presumed had died from exposure, how could he not?

The crunching sound in the snow that Bruce had learned to connect with someone or something approaching caught his attention. Like the animals that had mastered survival, Bruce stopped.

He squatted down to listen and wait. His ears had not failed him. He heard the gait of a man. Not just any man, but the confident walk that Bruce connected to Paul.

He wished he could see him, but the twelve rows of safety making Bruce invisible to Paul, also made Paul invisible to Bruce. Silence was now Bruce's best ally. He waited and counted steps. He estimated that each stride Paul took was about three feet. He paid close attention to the rhythm of the pace. He counted silently in his head.

He planned to allow Paul to move east another ten yards beyond the point where he could no longer hear him. He wished he had kept track of how far he had walked so he could calculate, using his watch, how many minutes he had before Paul reached his destination and then returned to the road.

Bruce knew that once Paul found out he had the clothes to warm his body, he'd speed up his return. He couldn't take the chance that Bruce might escape with a story to tell.

Paul's footsteps grew quiet.

Bruce counted as the distance between the men expanded to his projected ten yards. Confident that his calculations were correct, he started up again. The short break helped him to catch his breath and huddle down to conserve body heat.

He had to move quickly. He knew Paul's location and he knew the road was just ahead.

Even at the fastest pace Bruce could travel with his bad ankle, he was still only traveling half as fast as Paul at his slow, steady walk.

***

Paul's eyes scanned the tops of the cornstalks for his orange marker. He checked the tracks in the snow and knew he hadn't strayed from his path. His instincts told him the cap should be visible, but it wasn't.

He stopped to look behind him in case he had accidentally walked past it. He hadn't. He followed his own tracks further east still searching for that definitive spot of orange.

He stopped to look and listen. Something wasn't right. Could Bruce be waiting to ambush him again? Their first attempt had cost Drew his life. Surely, Bruce wouldn't be so stupid as to try again. What match is a hunting knife for a rifle?

Paul slid quietly to the south two rows over. He practiced his snake-like slithering through the corn, prepared to raise his rifle and fire at the slightest sign of Bruce.

Twenty yards later, he noticed the snow beneath his feet had signs of two men and lots of shuffling around. This must be where they had lain in wait for Paul to arrive. He had his bearings. He knew the scarecrow would be directly to his north, just two rows over.

He planned to snatch it up quickly then head west. He still assumed the weather had done his job for him, but he had learned a long time ago, never to rely one hundred percent on assumptions.

While rattlesnake hunting as a kid he *assumed* the snake he shot was dead. When he stepped forward to collect his trophy rattle, the snake struck out at him, catching his sleeve but not the skin beneath. From that day on, he vowed to always double check everything before acknowledging confirmation.

He eased his way through the last row. He stood over the spot where the scarecrow had been so strategically placed by the two hunters. He recognized the area, but there was no scarecrow. He looked over the tops of the cornstalks and there was no orange hat.

He squatted down to check the snow. After a closer examination of the ground he realized Bruce had dismantled the scarecrow, taking back his coat and boots. He must still be alive and moving.

Paul's breathing increased at the thought of Bruce getting away. He drew in a long, deep, breath and reminded himself to remain calm; rational decisions are never made out of anxiety or fear. Relaxation and alertness will take him to his missing prey.

His eyes scanned the ground for tracks that Bruce may have left behind. He found them. He moved into the row north of where he stood. He followed Bruce's tracks as they took the northern route across the rows. Tracking him was easy for Paul.

At the twelfth row he noticed Bruce had turned to the west.

"Damn," mumbled Paul.

Paul feared that Bruce had gotten his bearings after all, or at least was following a lucky hunch. Either way, he had a head start on Paul and he was headed in the right direction.

Paul turned to the west and jogged quickly down the furrow in search of his prey.

CHAPTER 35

Bruce kept his body moving west, but it slowed as he grew tired and out of breath again. Trying not to suck in too much cold air and dragging his foot, caused Bruce to expend way too much energy, increasing his fatigue, and allowing his body to grow chilled again.

Paul could tell by the tracks that Bruce needed to stop frequently. He could also tell that he was injured and possibly dragging a leg. He knew he would soon catch up to Bruce.

For Paul, the game lacked challenge.

Bruce was making his way back toward the road. He actually heard a vehicle drive past. He knew his freedom was close.

Finally, Paul could hear Bruce traveling through the corn. And, he knew that he was nearing the road. He stepped out of sight and watched from two rows away.

Bruce reached his two dead friends. He stopped and looked around, frantically searching for Paul. Paul had piled the bodies one on top of the other, like trash bags needing disposal. No dignity or respect for the men.

Bruce felt his stomach contents rising into his throat. The sight of the two dead men and knowing he could've been one of them caused him to vomit again.

Paul watched.

The blood rushed through Bruce's veins, nearly bursting his heart; the sound of the thumping deafened him. He trembled in fear. The road was in sight, the Escalade so close. Could he make a run for it, retrieve his shotgun, and put an end to this once and for all?

His eyes scanned the area for any sign of Paul. He knew Paul would have found out by then that Bruce had taken the coat and boots. He also knew at any second Paul could come bursting down the row behind him.

He had to make it to the Escalade before Paul returned. Armed he stood a chance. He wiped his tears, turned his eyes away from his dead friends, and stood to make that short run to the Escalade, the best run of his football career. Only a few yards, he knew he could do it.

He hoped his ankle wouldn't fail him. He practiced the numbers to his keypad in his head. Once he made it to the Escalade, he needed to punch in the numbers without hesitation.

Bruce stood tall and straight as he prepared for his run then drew in one long, deep breath. Taking one last look at the bodies of his friends, he said, "I'm going to make it right. I'm going to make him pay for what he did to you."

Bruce drew in another deep breath, filling his lungs for his short five-yard dash. He could see his Escalade clearly in the moonlit night. Four yards. Yes, he was going to make it. Three yards, he tasted the victory.

Thud.

All went dark. A .22 caliber bullet pierced his heart from behind.

CHAPTER 36

Paul had dropped him easily with just one shot. He stepped out from his hiding place to collect his final trophy. As he bent down to pick up Bruce's body from the ground, the sound of a cell phone ringing in the Escalade caught his attention.

He stopped and looked toward the vehicle then back to Bruce's body sprawled out face down in the snow and said, "Look's like you missed a phone call. Hope it wasn't important."

When the ringing stopped, Paul heaved Bruce's body onto his shoulder in the same manner he had carried Drew a short time before. He turned and walked back inside the cornfield. He added Bruce's body to the pile. He brushed the snow from his clothes and checked for bloodstains.

He casually strolled past the three bodies piled out of sight, just short of the road. He crossed the rows of corn, remaining hidden from the view of drivers passing by, to retrieve his own hidden pickup. The road, being so open, allowed him to see for a great distance. When there were no headlights approaching from either direction, he stepped out from the camouflage of the corn and walked in the ditch along the edge of the road where traveling on foot was easier than traveling through the corn.

As he walked he stopped to gaze up at the full moon. He loved living in the country, no city lights to block the view of the night sky. The stars appear brighter in Nebraska. The moon's glow was exceptionally spectacular that night. He wanted to soak in the splendor of Mother Nature.

He checked his watch—ten minutes past five. He'd better hurry if he didn't want to be late for dinner. He increased his pace to a slow jog, his favorite stride when going out to check the water tank in the pasture.

When he was a soldier in training, they were told to jog everywhere while on base or catch a ride, they were not to be seen walking during the day. With his tall, lean body and perfect health he had continued that jogging pace at some point every day since he left the war behind.

He found the trail road leading to the center pivot system and followed it to his parked pickup. He climbed into the bed of his pickup to rearrange the bales of hay he carried in the back during cold weather to use for traction if he found himself stuck in a snowdrift in a pasture or if his pickup accidentally slid off into a ditch. He stomped his feet before stepping inside—a bit of a clean freak, he didn't want snow and bits of broken leaves inside on the carpet or seats.

After giving the engine a few minutes to warm up, Paul adjusted his radio and pulled out into the intersection, where he eased his pickup slowly down the road—no need to turn on his headlights and attract attention. The full moon cast a blue glow over the landscape making it bright enough to allow full visibility of the road and the adjacent fields.

He kept his eyes on the rearview mirror. If he spotted lights from an approaching vehicle, he'd just keep moving to the corner and turn out of sight and then return when he felt it was safe.

No lights behind him, or in front of him, meant no traffic was near. The long, straight, flat country roads allowed him to see for more than a mile in both directions.

He parked next to the not so shiny, red Escalade. The town's streets filled with slush and snow created a muddy mixture that had splashed onto the sides. He stepped out and stretched, raising his right arm over his head and then his left. He turned his neck over each shoulder. He felt and heard small pops and snaps. He cracked his knuckles then moved inside the corn to retrieve the bodies.

Paul threw Bruce over his shoulder and walked the short distance to his pickup. He tossed Bruce's body into the bed on top of the rubber mat used to protect the paint while hauling fence posts and wire and other farmer/rancher tools of the trade.

He scanned the road again. Next, he pulled Drew's body up onto his shoulder and carried him to the bed of the pickup. He had taken the time to plan his load. He had placed Bruce's body, head toward the cab, feet toward the tailgate with his body pressed to the driver's side wheel well. He dropped Drew's body closely against Bruce.

Again, he checked for privacy then return to the cornfield for his first kill of the day, Rick. His body was colder and stiffer than the last two making it a little more difficult to maneuver, but he managed.

The three bodies were packed into the bed of his pickup like sardines in a can. Three strangers, whom Paul knew nothing about beyond their misfortune of the day, had offered him a retreat from his boredom, a sort of reminder that he still had the ability to stalk and win a battle against the enemy.

Paul stepped out onto the road to stand at a higher elevation than the ditch where he had parked his pickup. He relieved himself on the road while he scanned for oncoming vehicles. Still no one appeared. He returned to his pickup.

Always prepared, he carried a blanket behind the seat, along with a flashlight, a small, flat toolbox under the seat, a roll of paper towels and a few chocolate bars in the event he became stranded along the side of the road and had to either walk for help or wait patiently for a neighbor to drive by.

He removed the blanket and shook it open. It floated high into the air and spread out over the bodies. He then broke open one of the timothy grass hay bales, sprinkling the thin-bladed grass hay over the blanket, he completely and thoroughly covered his kill.

The bed of his pickup looked as though it contained loose hay ready to feed his cattle. No sign of the blanket or the men in view. Proud of his work, he returned to the cab.

Again, he stomped his feet and brushed tiny bits of hay from his clothes, but before entering, he slid the seat forward again and removed a Hershey bar from his stash.

He climbed into the pickup and unwrapped his chocolate. He enjoyed the creamy sensation of the chocolate melting in his mouth. He turned on his headlights and eased his way onto the road. It was time to go home.

CHAPTER 37

Slowly, Paul drove toward home. He kept his speed slow to avoid the hay flying out from the bed of the pickup, exposing his hidden stash. He fidgeted with his radio until he found a song that pleased him. His focus returned to his chocolate bar as he separated each of the tiny squares of chocolate, one by one, and let them melt slowly in his mouth.

As he made his way closer to his farm, he met several neighbors on their way home from town, ready for dinner. They honked or waved as soon as they saw Paul.

Luckily for him, not one of those neighbors had been on the road just a few minutes earlier. Certainly, one of them would've stopped to offer assistance had they seen him pulled over in the ditch along the edge of the deserted road.

Paul hadn't taken the time to plan his story if a friend or neighbor had stopped to help. Making a mental note that no one showed up earlier to help the hunters, or turn in the missing Escalade, or interfere with Paul's afternoon hunt, he felt more convinced than ever that the hunters had sealed their own destiny earlier in the day.

Finally, one of Paul's neighbors, Keith, stopped him.

"Hi, Paul. What's up?"

"Thought I'd do a little hunting."

"Did you get any birds?"

"As a matter of fact I did."

Paul stepped out of his pickup and walked to the back.

He turned to see Keith had left his pickup to join him.

Paul reached into the bed just behind the window, next to the remaining, unopened, bales of hay, to retrieve the birds the hunters had shot earlier in the day at his farm.

"I guess I haven't lost my touch," said Paul. "Do you want them?"

"Why?" asked Keith. "Don't you?"

"Nah, I don't like cleanin' them and Liz doesn't like cookin' them. So, if you want them, go ahead and help yourself."

"Gee thanks, Paul. I love to eat pheasant. I'll enjoy these for lunch tomorrow."

The two men leaned against the bed of the pickup and chatted for a bit then Paul said, "Well, I've got animals to feed. I'd better head home."

"Yeah, me too. Thanks again for the birds. You have a good evening now."

Each man returned to the cab of his pickup and nodded a courtesy nod then the two vehicles parted ways.

Paul did not appear to be even slightly uncomfortable having three dead bodies in the bed of his pickup. He actually enjoyed the thrill of having someone so close to finding out.

His thoughts turned to the scene if it had gone differently. What would he have done if the wind would've shifted the fine grass hay and exposed his secret? He would've had no choice but to kill Keith if he had discovered the bodies. What else could he do? He liked Keith, but not enough to go to prison. What difference does it make killing one more after he already had three dead men in the bed of his pickup.

Keith's unfortunate death would have cost him a little more time and inconvenience but he could've handled the situation and the extra body. He was pleased that the bodies went undiscovered, saving him that extra time and trouble.

With less than a half mile remaining before he arrived at his farm, he didn't expect further unplanned interruptions. Rather than pulling into his driveway next to his house, he drove to the back road leading to the rear of the west barn.

The full moon continued to assist him and guide his way. Behind his barn was an area where he ground silage, a form of fermented feed produced from high moisture corn, for his cattle.

He jogged from his pickup to his tractor—an older John Deere tractor with a front-end loader that he had purchased at a used farm equipment sale. The John Deere Company's bright yellow and green trademark paint had long since oxidized, and rust eased its way onto the frame.

He no longer farmed his land, so he only used the old tractor for moving feed around his farm. It didn't bother him that the green and yellow paint had long ago faded and the rusted scratches didn't affect the way it ran. He was proud of the money he had saved when he purchased it.

Paul's wife, Liz, was appalled by the appearance of the old worn tractor. Paul had more than enough money to buy several brand new tractors, priced at over two hundred thousand dollars each. He had no intention of squandering his hard-earned money on a luxury tractor that had a nice paint job. His frugal ways had helped him reach the financial security that Liz took for granted.

He started his tractor and, using the front-end loader, he picked up a twelve hundred pound round bale of hay, dropping it into the large orange and black Rotogrind tub grinder. The tall, round canister contained metal blades called hammers that spun loosely, and the shear plates were set for a fine cut, chopping all of the contents into tiny bits smaller than a dime.

He returned to his pickup and lifted the blanket far enough to expose the legs of the three bodies. One by one, he grabbed the men just above the ankles and pulled them out onto the ground. Their bodies hit the ground with a loud thud.

Next, he removed his freshly sharpened pocketknife that sliced easily through the fabric of the hunting clothes on the bodies. After he had cut the clothing from his three victims, he tossed the clothes onto the ground. Next, he piled the naked bodies, one atop the other, in a heap, much the same way he had piled them earlier in the cornfield. He had arms, legs, and heads facing different directions helping them to balance more easily.

He jogged back to the tractor and climbed aboard. Turning the tractor toward the pickup, he inched forward. Lowering the front-end loader to the ground with amazing precision, he scooped the bodies into the bucket of the loader.

He turned the tractor and moved it closer to the top of the tub grinder. Then, ever so carefully, he slowly raised the bucket. An arm fell limp over the edge of the bucket. The tangled mass of bodies, with arms and legs interwoven, helped keep them secure inside the bucket. As a precaution, not wanting to lose any of his precious cargo, he performed each step in slow motion until, finally, he had them positioned over the top of the tub grinder. Tipping the bucket, they dropped silently onto the top of the hay already in the grinder.

CHAPTER 38

While the mixture of naked men and hay churned, Paul stepped just inside his barn and returned with a white, plastic, woven grain bag. He shoved the hunters' clothing into the bag. He had to force the last jacket inside, having filled the bag to capacity. He carried that bag out from the pasture behind the barn, through the gate, in full view of the house. He made his way to a homemade incinerator in his backyard.

He had fashioned livestock wire fencing, with four-inch squares, into a double-wrapped circle. He used that for burning trash from the house or small branches and twigs that the old Chinese elm trees shed on windy days.

He tossed the bag containing the clothing—the last bit of evidence— into his burn ring. The night sky caught

Cornstalked

his attention once again. He stepped out from the spot where he was standing to take in a wider view.

Realizing time was slipping away, he returned to his task and lit the contents of the ring—a combination of that morning's trash from the house and the grain bag—with the wooden stick matches he always carried in his jacket pocket.

A bit of a firebug, Paul burned trash and branches daily—partly because he liked to keep the area around his property clean and tidy, and partly because he liked the sight, sound, and smell of a roaring fire.

Sometimes the flames flicker and go out before the entire contents of the ring have burned down to nothing but ashes. Tonight, he stood a vigilant watch over the fire. He searched the ground for a branch that he could use to stir the contents.

Snow had concealed any branches that may have escaped his eye the day before. He walked back to the barn and returned with a four-tined pitchfork that he used daily to pitch hay to the horses.

The day's debris from the house, being mostly paper, had quickly turned to ashes. The clothing burned more slowly, especially the boots. Concerned they might not disappear the way he had hoped; he walked to his tool shed for a metal can filled with gasoline. He doused the fire with the flammable liquid and the flames shot high above the top of the wire for a short time.

He stirred the mixture once again and waited. He decided no one would be out looking for the men that night. In the morning, when the ashes had cooled, he would remove anything that was left unburned and stow it away until he could bury the last bit of evidence of his crime in the soft, wet soil of springtime.

Paul carried his pitchfork over his shoulder as he walked back to his barn. In the glow of the moonlight, his silhouette carrying the pitchfork rivaled that of the devil himself. He set the pitchfork just inside the door against the wall then turned off the light. Then he walked back to his pickup and climbed in.

He carefully backed under the conveyer spout of the grinder. Then he walked to the side of the grinder and turned on the conveyor that blew the contents out of the spout. He stood back out of the cloud of dust created by the dry hay, and watched as the mixture poured into the bed of his pickup.

He slid back onto the seat of his pickup and inched it forward, watching out the rear window to be certain to catch all of the contents, allowing not even the tiniest amount to fall to the ground. Satisfied that he had performed a clean and tidy job of collecting the flowing concoction, he returned to the grinder and turned it off.

It wasn't far to the pasture where he kept his cattle behind the house. He eased his pickup across the snowy road to the gate. The sound of his pickup entering the

Cornstalked

pasture caused the always-hungry cattle to appear from out of the darkness.

He stepped out of the pickup while the engine remained running. It cruised at a slow speed of five miles per hour through the pasture. Paul climbed into the back and shoveled out the contents—a mixture of hay and dead bodies chopped so fine and mixed together so well that no one, even the cattle, would notice. The morbid feed mixture fell onto the ground in a straight line as it did every time he fed ground hay to the cattle.

Sweeping the last bit out of the bed of the pickup, Paul jumped down and ran alongside his pickup then climbed in.

The hungry, unsuspecting cattle quickly downed the evening feed. Lined out in the light of the moon, three hundred head of Black Angus cattle stood side-by-side in two rows, disposing of the remains of the three strangers.

CHAPTER 39

Paul whistled his no particular melody whistle as he pulled into the driveway of his home. He pressed the garage door opener then parked inside. As the door closed, he slipped out of his vehicle. He stomped his feet and brushed the bits of feed from his clothing.

Inside, Liz met him at the door.

"Where've you been?"

"Doin' chores and feeding the cattle. What's for supper?"

"That's it? What's for supper? I told you about what those men did to us and you just walked out of here like nothing happened. I can't believe you. Don't you have any compassion at all? What kind of man would allow those guys to get away with what they did?"

Cornstalked

Without an answer, he went into the bathroom to wash his hands and face for dinner.

Too angry to join him for the meal, Liz stormed off to their room.

Peggy served the steaming hot chili soup, a bowl of oyster crackers, and a block of cheddar cheese sliced into rectangular pieces on a cheese board.

Paul looked across the table at Peggy and said, "You alright?"

"Yes," she answered quietly.

She always hated it when her parents fought. Actually, her mom did all of the fighting and yelling. Her dad would just walk away, or leave the house completely, which infuriated her mother even more. On occasion, Liz might even throw a few things, pillows, towels, pots, and sometimes dishes or coffee mugs. But Peggy's dad always remained calm. If her mom followed him outside, he'd just get into his pickup and leave. Much like he did earlier that day.

Paul stirred the chili, with bits of meat, beans, and onions smaller than a dime, swimming in the hot tomato broth. He waited for it to cool sufficiently before taking his first spoonful. Peggy and her dad ate their meal in silence.

CHAPTER 40

Saturday late afternoon:

After Charlie left Paul's property to continue his investigation regarding the missing hunters, Paul strolled back into his barn. He pulled the frayed collar of his jean jacket up around his neck. The old stone barn offered shelter from the wind, but certainly couldn't keep out the frigid fall air.

When the last stall was picked clean, he leaned the pitchfork against the south wall and headed out the door. Without looking, his hand reached up as he walked from the barn, and turned off the light switch, just as he had done several times every day for several decades. Paul's

Cornstalked

life was made up of dozens of daily habits and tasks grouped together like links in a chain.

Daily routines, daily chores, daily boredom at times, but then the past twenty-four hours were far from boring as he thought about the hunters who were now the subject of a frantic search and rescue.

Before entering his garage, Paul stomped his feet, shaking bits of straw and hay from his clothes, the same as any other day. He walked in, hung his hat and coat on the pegs near the door, and went into the bathroom to wash up for dinner.

Paul sat at the table to join Liz and Peggy. Saturday nights were taco nights at their house. Paul filled a soft, flour tortilla with pinto beans, seasoned ground beef, shredded lettuce, and cheddar cheese.

Peggy and Liz preferred the hard-shell, white corn taco shells.

"Did you make any guacamole?" asked Paul.

"Not tonight. The avocadoes at the store were too hard," said Liz.

"How about a little sour cream then?" he asked.

"I'll get it," said Peggy.

"Well?" asked Liz.

"Well what?" asked Paul, his mouth filled with beans.

"What did Charlie want?"

"He asked me if I saw a red Escalade drive by," said Paul.

"What did you tell him?" asked Liz.

"The truth. The whole truth, and nothing but the truth, so help me God," said Paul with a twinkle in his eye.

That twinkle was one of his best assets. That twinkle had stolen Liz's heart when she was a young teenage girl. She assumed that sparkle had disappeared forever.

"What?" asked Peggy. "I don't get it."

"That's how they swear you in when you're going to testify in court," explained Liz.

Liz smiled at Paul.

"You're in a good mood tonight," she said.

"Yep. Life is good," he responded.

"Dad, why did Charlie want to know about the red, whatever?" asked Peggy.

"I guess some hunters are missing," he said. "Can you pass me that sour cream now?"

"Missing?" asked Peggy. "How can anyone be missing out here? There's always someone to give you a ride if you need help."

She handed the unopened container of sour cream to her dad.

"Charlie said they found their SUV but they weren't in it," said Paul.

Cornstalked

He opened the container of sour cream and dipped his spoon into it, coming out with a large blob that he carefully added to the inside of his taco before squeezing it closed.

"Were they locals?" asked Liz.

"I don't have all the details," said Paul. He sipped from his water glass. "Just that there were three hunters in the SUV and they don't know where they wandered off to."

Liz put her taco down.

"Three hunters?"

"Yep," said Paul. He wiped his chin to catch a drip from the meat.

"And you say they're missing?" she asked.

"Yes, I thought that part was clear by now," he answered.

Her mind raced back to the previous day when her husband had left her and Peggy alone while he went into town and the three hunters appeared in their corrals out of nowhere.

She looked solemnly down into her plate. What were they driving? Had she seen their vehicle? How had they left, on foot or did they drive away?

"What's wrong with you?" asked Paul.

"Could they be those three men who were here yesterday?" she asked.

"I told you never to talk about them again," said Paul.

Liz looked at Paul across the table. His attitude about the three men from the day before set her off in an angry sort of way.

"That's it?" asked Liz. "I told you what those three men did, and all you can do is tell us to forget it ever happened? What kind of a husband and father are you?"

Paul looked into Peggy's confused eyes. He stood up, pushed in his chair, and went off to his den without finishing his dinner.

"Mom. What'd you do that for?" asked Peggy.

"Do what?"

"Make Dad mad like that?"

"He made me mad," said Liz.

"Why should you be mad?" asked Peggy.

"I don't like his reaction to those men being here yesterday," said Liz in an angry tone. "We could've been killed."

"But we weren't killed," said Peggy. "Besides, I heard what you told Dad."

"What do you mean, what I told your dad?"

"I heard you tell him how those men broke into the house and attacked us," said Peggy.

"That's right and did you see what your father did? He left. He didn't seem to care at all."

Cornstalked

"Didn't it occur to you when you made up that story about the men breaking in here that he knew all along you were lying?"

CHAPTER 41

Five months later:

The case of the missing hunters had turned cold. With no clues or evidence whatsoever, beyond the red Escalade and their luggage at the motel, to assist in the investigation and search, it was as if they had never stepped foot into Perkins County.

When the spring thaw arrived, Paul had ridden out to the sand hills on horseback carrying a white, woven, plastic, grain bag filled with ashes and bits of leather and buckles. He found a spot near an old, pink, wild rose bush—a rare find on the prairie. The fragrance is far more intense than any of the new man-made varieties of roses.

Cornstalked

Paul frequently stopped at this bush to pick a rose and enjoy the sweet fragrance throughout the day.

He climbed down from his pale palomino horse, and removed the posthole digger that he had strapped to the back of his saddle. He dug a hole three feet straight down and only wide enough to force the bag down into—about ten inches wide. That way he disturbed the least amount of sand in such a way as not to draw anyone's attention to the hole.

He forced the bag into the narrow opening in the prairie soil then filled it back in with the loose sand that he had carefully piled next to the hole in one tidy mound, again trying to keep the spot looking undisturbed.

Glancing around, he found a flat sandstone, slightly larger in diameter than the hole he had dug. He pried it loose and set it atop the hole. He picked up a handful of old dried grass and swept the sand clean where the stone once sat.

He knew with wind in the forecast that any footprints he left behind would disappear in a matter of minutes. Paul's secret would remain sealed in the land.

Fall almost one year after the hunters arrived:

When fall arrived, Peggy went away to the University of Nebraska at Lincoln, Nebraska.

Liz had filed for divorce when she was faced with spending the rest of her life living with Paul without their daughter. She followed Peggy to Lincoln, where she started a new life.

Paul still woke early every morning, went outside to tend to his livestock then came in for a bowl of cold cereal, a slice of toast without butter, and a small glass of orange juice.

He still drove into town at ten o'clock every morning to join the other men for a cup of coffee and a donut. His routine had remained untouched.

Denver:

Kimberly Clarke woke every morning and thanked the universe for her wonderful new life. Bruce's body had never been recovered. He had left behind a three million dollar life insurance policy. She had assumed he was insured, but had no idea what the policy was worth.

He had taken out the life insurance policy through the bank where he worked. Most of the employees insured themselves from fifty thousand to one hundred thousand; some even went as high as a quarter of a million dollars. But Bruce always felt he was worth so much more than the average person, and he had insured himself with that thought in mind.

Cornstalked

The insurance company contacted Kimberly when Bruce was presumed dead. The only act of kindness he had performed during their relationship was to write her name down on the policy as sole beneficiary to his entire estate. His estate consisted of the home they lived in with the unpaid mortgage, and his shiny red Escalade that he had only made a few payments on, aside from that, his personal belongings such as clothes and sports equipment.

Kimberly chose to keep the house, but removed all of Bruce's clothing and personal items. She hired an interior decorator to change his office from floor to ceiling so that when it was finished she wouldn't recognize it as having once been Bruce's office. As a matter of fact, she refused to step foot inside until the decorator had informed her that it was finished.

Aside from thanking the universe for her new life, she had daily chores that gave her great joy. Feeding the fish in her rather large aquarium filled with saltwater fish that had turned her living room into an underwater wonderland was the perfect way to start her day.

She smiled while she watched her Siamese cat stand on the chair near the aquarium swatting at the fish as they swam around the tank. She'd grab a quick cup of coffee then head out the door with her matched pair of Doberman Pinchers on leashes, anxious for their morning walk.

Although Bruce was presumed dead, since his body had never been found, she felt safe with her two large companions in the event he would return unannounced and attempt to break into her home. She had changed the locks soon after the search and rescue efforts ended.

Her life of terror was replaced by joy and happiness, with no plans for a man in her immediate future.

CORNSTALKED was originally written as a short story. Patricia was encouraged by her readers to expand the short story into a full-length novel. CORNSTALKED, the novel, is also available as an e-book. Fifty percent of the sales from the e-book version will be donated to Domestic Abuse Programs. Ten percent of the sale of CORNSTALKED, from the author's website, www.patriciabremmer.com,will also be donated.

The short story is attached to this book as an added feature. Enjoy!

CORNSTALKED

The cool, crisp fall air bit the flesh on Paul's
weathered face as he stepped outside for morning chores.
He drew a deep breath, filling his lungs, holding on to it
momentarily, like a smoker taking in the full effect of the
nicotine before releasing it. His eyes surveyed with pride
the acres of land filled with horses and cattle—a self-made
man, spawned from simple roots, now worth several
million. Not that anyone would notice by his plain
rancher attire. He zipped his vest, being careful not to
break the threads in the old, worn zipper. His wife, Liz,
had warned him that if he brought it to her one more time
for repairs she would toss it in the trash. He rarely
bought new clothes, wearing his old shirts until they were
threadbare, more comfortable he always said. He
buttoned his snug-fitting jean jacket, also showing years
of wear, especially around the cuffs where the white
threads frayed and hung down around his gloved hands
while he fixed fence. With a brisk pace and a slight jog to
his step, he went to the barns to feed his horses. He
watched as the magnificent animals raced to their feed

bunks from the pasture, kicking their hind legs high into the air. Dodging the dangerous hooves was second nature to this ex-war veteran who spent his entire life, outside of the war, working with horses and cattle.

His soft blue eyes squinted in the morning sun, exaggerating the deep wrinkles extending out from the corners, as he examined every inch of the animals while they gathered around to feed. Content that every one appeared to be in good flesh and void of injuries from rough play, he continued on his way. He reminisced of the time when his chores were done solely on horseback, but having grown older, he joined the ranks of younger farmers and ranchers using pickups for their daily rounds. Seated in his pickup, waiting for the engine to warm, he tuned the radio to Paul Harvey's *The Rest of the Story*. He pampered his pickup much the same way he cared for his livestock. Too bad his wife lacked the same respect. Liz rarely saw signs of affection from the man who swept her off her feet seventeen years earlier. Her transformation to wife and mother caused him to look at her differently, treat her differently, and love her differently. Disappointed, she learned to tolerate the change. She so desperately yearned for the man she married, a man who showed her passion. She grew to understand that the stern tyrant he had for a mother, although he respected her, left him with a bitter feeling toward any woman who reminded him of his childhood years. Now, Liz became a version of his mother. He preferred spending time outdoors with his animals, where he encouraged his daughter to join him at every opportunity. He was a gentle father who loved to teach her everything he knew about the animals. It was his knowledge and care of these animals that made him a wealthy man.

He whistled gently to himself, a habit he developed long ago as a stress release, as he eased the pickup along the lengthy driveway to the road's edge. He hesitated when he noticed a bright red pickup slowly approaching. Hunters, he thought. He didn't have much use for hunters. He had long ago given up his desire to kill animals. When he was a boy, he hunted every time the opportunity presented itself. Sometimes he'd finish his chores and stay out past dark with his dogs and horse. During the war, his exposure to death changed him. He left an innocent farm boy and returned a grown man with a new view on human life.

The shiny, red Escalade, now splattered with mud and snow from the country roads, eased to a stop. A young man in his thirties, literally dressed to kill, stepped out. Paul always wondered why city hunters thought they needed to spend hundreds of dollars on camouflaged clothing, with heavy boots, orange vests, and matching hats. Why, when he was a boy, he rode bareback and barefoot while he hunted rabbits. He rolled down his window to hear what the eager stranger had to say.

"Excuse me sir, would you mind if we hunted your trees?" asked Bruce, showing his perfect smile, recently whitened.

"I'd rather you didn't," came the response from Paul, his voice so soft it was barely audible.

"You say, you'd rather we didn't?" asked the hunter, thinking he might have misunderstood him. He had just spotted at least two-dozen birds in his trees. Surely, this guy wasn't keeping them all for himself.

"That's right," Paul cleared his throat. "I'd rather you didn't."

"Can I ask why?" persisted the young man.

"I have horses and cattle and I don't want anyone hurt from an accident."

"I can guarantee, you won't have anything to worry about," said the hunter smugly.

"That's right, I won't," murmured Paul, "because you're not hunting on my property."

He rolled up his window, pulled onto the road, and drove north out of view from the hunters.

Feeling angry and defeated, Bruce kicked his boot in the gravel on the road as he gnawed the inside of his lower lip. As the president of his bank in Denver, he was unaccustomed to anyone standing up to him or disagreeing. In high school, the leadership role fit him well, starting with the position of captain of the football team. Everyone, including the teachers and staff, looked up to him, and his team members followed his lead from one victory to the next, creating an over-inflated ego. Even his wife learned early on to avoid conflict, just give in. He felt reluctant to return to his friends defeated.

"Did he tell you no?" asked Rick.

"Yeah, the old goat wants to keep all the birds to himself."

"Where should we go from here?" asked Drew, the driver, as he leaned forward over the steering wheel to talk with Bruce.

Bruce walked alongside the SUV, kicking the tires and thinking. He turned toward the house that Paul had left and relieved himself on the road, marking his territory, signaling the fight was on. The sound of several pheasants flapping their wings and cackling as they flew to join the others in the trees turned his attention away from the house.

"You know what? The hell with him. He doesn't own the birds. Who in the hell does he think he is? Pull around behind the house and let's walk the trees."

The two men in the Escalade didn't dare question his decision. They backed down the gravel road until they came to the intersection of a trail road and the main road. With trees lining both sides of the trail, they felt confident they were completely hidden from view. The sun shone brightly on the crusted snow, creating a glare that required sunglasses to protect their eyes from the burn. The three men gathered around the back of the Escalade and passed around their bottle of Jack Daniels before starting the trek through the trees. Spending most of their time in their offices at the bank hadn't prepared them for the cold temperatures surrounding them. Being slightly overweight from lack of exercise, their bellies extending over their belt lines forced them to buy coats slightly larger than their frame required just to cover them, which made walking more difficult.

The bottle made one more round before they ventured off into the tree row. Over the years, the old trees had shed branches from storms and decay creating thick underbrush that made perfect cover for the pheasants and other small wildlife. Each step caused their weight to snap branches, alerting the nearby pheasants that immediately took flight away from the hunters. Several birds flew up from only three feet away. The startled men raised their shotguns and fired. The sound echoed through the trees and they watched as several more birds took flight.

Rick, the youngest of the three, fancied himself as the pretty boy, the one the women couldn't resist, although no one had taken the time to explain that to the women he met. He suggested, "Maybe we should walk the trail road to the end and then turn around and walk the trees, sending the birds closer to the Escalade. That way when we hit the birds we won't have as far to carry them."

Anything to avoid excess exercise, the others agreed.

Trudging along the path, where no vehicle had gone since the snow fell; they found themselves breathlessly struggling to advance in the deep snow. At the end of the trail road, they stopped to rest. Looking back, they realized they'd only walked less than half a mile. Hot, sweating, and out of breath, they still had to return to where they had begun, only this time they had to be prepared to react quickly to drop the birds as they rose above the ground.

Drew took off his backpack and removed the bottle of Jack Daniels. He took a long drink then passed it to his friends. With only beef jerky for breakfast and several hours of swigging on the now nearly empty bottle, the effects of the alcohol became apparent. They stood, faltering from the combination of fatigue from their walk and the booze. They moved into the thick underbrush of the trees and headed back. Birds took flight all around them. They shot carelessly into the air, missing every bird. The sound of the branches cracking from the pellets released from the shotgun shells filled the air. They continued east toward their vehicle. When they were only fifty feet from the Escalade, a flock of birds took to the air again. They fired.

7

"I got one!" yelled Bruce.

"Me too," said Rick excitedly.

They ran clumsily in the directions the birds had fallen. When they reached the pickup along the way, Bruce groaned, "One of you bastards hit my Escalade. Look at it." The front end sported a broken headlight and the spray of the pellets chipped the shiny, red paint, exposing the drab gray primer.

"I'm going after my bird," said Rick as he darted through the trees and over the fence into the rancher's corrals.

"I can't find it!" he yelled.

The other two joined him. They wandered through the corrals looking for the downed birds in clear view of the house.

Peggy called out, "Mom, hurry! I think those are hunters in with the horses!"

Liz rushed to the window to check it out, hoping she was wrong.

Suddenly, several of the horses burst into the corral running at full speed, bucking and playing, hoping the humans were about to feed them again. The men darted for the safety of the fences, stumbling and falling on the way. Bruce rolled over onto his back, raised his shotgun, and took aim at one of the horses racing toward him.

Liz and Peggy held their breath. They turned away, waiting for the horrible sound of one of their prized animals being shot by the trespasser.

The horse pivoted and turned away at the last second.

"Call Dad," said Peggy.

"I can't. My phone's in my purse and my purse is in the car next to the corral fence."

The men climbed over the fence then dropped to the ground on the other side, laughing at their near escape from the deadly horses. Again, they passed around the bottle.

Drew faced the house. As he tipped back his head for the last swallow, he noticed the two figures standing in the window, watching them.

"Hey, take a gander at the babes. Wanna have a little fun?"

"Hell, why not?" said Rick.

They sprang to their feet then ran toward the house, stopped and loaded their guns in front of the two frightened residents. Surrounding the house, shooting into the air and laughing, they searched for an open door.

After they finished with the women, they stumbled back through the trees, found their Escalade, and drove away. Seconds after they pulled out onto the road, they met Paul returning home, so they honked, waved, and saluted him.

9

"Drunken city bastards," he said in his soft tone.

He knew they had defied him by hunting in his trees. His eyes slowly scanned the corrals to look for an injured horse. Then he noticed a red shell casing on his driveway. He rushed inside.

Liz and Peggy rushed to his arms for comfort and protection.

"What happened?' he asked, his quiet voice grew firm.

"Those men, oh Paul, what they did to us!"

"What'd they do?"

Liz sent Peggy out of the room. She hid behind the door and listened as her mother described how the men had broken into the house and assaulted them.

He pulled away from Liz, not quite knowing how to deal with female tears.

"You don't look like you're hurt too bad. You'll be fine," he said as he walked out to the barn to check his horses. He found two dead pheasants in the weeds under the corral fence. He carried the limp bodies to his pickup and tossed them into the back then he climbed in and drove away.

He cruised down the country roads until he spotted the red Escalade parked along the edge of a cornfield. Rick stood near the SUV while Bruce and Drew had gone deep into the rows to frighten the birds out toward Rick, who hoped to quickly drop his limit.

Paul drove past, while the drunken Rick, not recognizing him, waved. He pulled onto a maintenance road leading to the center pivot for the sprinkler system, used for watering the crop. He slowly and methodically slipped out of his pickup, tipped the seat forward, and removed his always-loaded .22-caliber rifle. Easing his way toward the man instinctively brought back Paul's training as a soldier. He easily approached the man without being seen. He raised his rifle and fired, dropping the hunter in one shot.

Bruce and Drew heard the gunshot and rushed toward Rick, anxious to see if he shot a bird. What they saw ahead of them, down the row, stopped them dead in their tracks. They felt their hearts beating hard in their chests as they watched Paul drag the lifeless body of their fellow hunter into the corn. They remained frozen, hoping Paul would just leave without finding them. Holding their breath, they watched as Paul returned to their Escalade, removed the keys, and locked the doors.

"What the hell," whispered Bruce. "That bastard's crazy."

For some insane reason, they felt if they remained motionless, he wouldn't see them. They watched in fear.

Paul stood tall, adjusted his hat and jacket then moved into the cornfield. His soft blue eyes, transformed into a steely gray, looked directly at them.

The two frightened hunters scrambled out of view. They tried to cross the rows of corn without being noticed, but the high ridges and deep snow caused them to stumble and fall, breaking cornstalks, or at least causing them to rustle and sway, alerting a keen eye to their location.

Paul had a keen eye, and keen hearing. Having spent most of his life in the country, and maneuvering cornfields in search of birds or coyotes, his gait was smooth and steady. With his rifle barrel perched against his shoulder, he whistled quietly as he walked. Soon the figure of a man, the man who without the least sign of remorse, shot and killed their companion in cold blood, disappeared into the tall corn.

Bruce and Drew had managed to stay close to each other, not that they could do anything to protect each other against a man with a rifle. Not just any man, but a heartless man with military training. Not planning to shoot birds, but rather flush them for Rick, they thought it easier to transverse the cornrows unarmed. An oversight they soon regretted.

One wrong move, one hasty step into the rows, would cause the dried leaves to release a sound pinpointing their location. Fear sobered them, reducing the courage that Jack Daniels had provided earlier. Their adrenaline raced. Sweat beaded on their foreheads. Frightened and full of liquor, they both needed to relieve

12

themselves, but how could they? The sound of them urinating could cost them their lives. They crouched down close to the ground, their hearts pounding in their ears, their bladders feeling as if they would soon burst, causing them to die a slow death. They knew they had to have a plan, some way to outwit this man. Maybe they should talk about which of them should die for the other. If Paul was distracted in pursuit of one of them, the other could flee to safety. One more life would be lost, but their assailant would be brought to justice. That had to be worth something.

"What should we do?" whispered Drew, hoping Bruce, who always had an answer for everything, would have one now.

"Shhh," said Bruce.

"Do you have your phone?" asked Drew.

"No, it's in the Escalade. Yours?"

"In the Escalade."

The crunching sound of dried cornstalks warned them as Paul drew nearer.

"I can't believe we left our guns behind," whispered Drew.

Paul was close enough they could hear his quiet whistle.

"We'd better get moving," whispered Bruce.

Slowly, the two men eased away from the sound of Paul's footsteps.

A master hunter, he paused to watch and wait.

The two men tried to walk while squatting down, but they made no progress, falling over onto the ground with each step. They rose up slightly and moved forward.

Paul caught a glimpse of their orange hats. "Morons," he mumbled.

He watched for a few seconds as the two bright orange heads bobbed up and down across the rows.

"They couldn't live one day at war," he spoke quietly, as if he were speaking to another soldier on patrol with him. Had his mind slipped back to kill or be killed from his tour of duty?

He fired in their direction.

The top of a cornstalk bent in two from the hit by the .22 bullet.

The two terrified men forced their eyes to penetrate the rows of corn in search of Paul so they'd know which direction to move.

Of course, he was dressed in a light brown jacket with a tan cap, making him invisible against the cornstalks.

Slowly, they crawled on their hands and knees; rough ground beneath the snow sliced their wrists, highlighting their path with red droplets on the snow. Broken cornstalks cut the exposed flesh on their faces. They brushed the red snow, smearing the blood into a bright pink. It didn't matter, even without the blood, or the indentations and drag marks left behind, Paul could easily find them.

They crawled for what seemed like a mile, although it had been less than a quarter of the distance. The fear and anxiety of being lost in a cornfield always causes a panicked person to misgauge their direction and distance. The sun had disappeared when the sky grew overcast. Surely, they'd come to the end of a row and find a road or a house or someone to help them from this madman who had killed their friend.

That might have been possible had they just followed a row to the end, but they continued to cross rows, failing to walk in a straight line. They weaved back and forth, increasing their time but not shortening their distance.

They stopped to rest again.

Paul, knowing their location, passed them a few rows over and now stood ahead of them while they looked back toward the direction they had come. A shot rang out, and once again, a cornstalk above their heads broke and fell to the ground. The two men scattered in opposite directions, playing into Paul's plan. His intention all along was to separate them. He could've hit them with his first two shots, but he enjoyed the taunting game, much like a cat with a mouse. He sensed their fear; it hung heavy in the air. The feeling of being stalked and all alone intensified it. That second shot, so close, caused them to empty their full, aching bladders. A wind had moved in, and without the sun, they would soon chill from their wet clothes.

Paul knew he planned to kill them. They knew he planned to kill them, but they wondered how much longer their luck would hold out. However, this wasn't about luck, it was more about the chase, the exhilaration for a man who lived such a peaceful, non-eventful life in his small, rural town.

He knew it was necessary to take his time, necessary for daylight to fade before he could finish. Slowly and methodically, he tracked Drew. It was easy. He followed the sound of his breathing, his feet crunching the dried vegetation, and when that failed, the pheasants that were scared up as he approached.

After another hour had passed, he tired of the chase and moved in for the kill. He positioned himself, once again, ahead of his prey. He waited, spotted an orange vest, took aim, and dropped Drew. He had orchestrated his chase to herd his victim closer to the edge of the field where the game had begun. He checked for a pulse then squatted down and threw the man over his shoulder as if he were carrying a bag of grain, a daily chore. He dropped him on top of his first kill of the day then went in search of Bruce.

The game lacked challenge. Bruce had accidentally begun to make his way back toward the road.

Paul stepped out of sight and watched from two rows away. Bruce reached his two dead friends. He stopped and looked around, frantically searching for Paul.

His blood rushed through his veins nearly bursting his heart; the sound of the thumping deafened him. He trembled in fear. The road was in sight, the Escalade so close. Could he make a run for it, break a window to retrieve his shotgun, and put an end to this once and for all? At least armed he stood a chance. He wiped his tears, turned his eyes away from his dead friends, and stood to make that short run to the Escalade, the best run of his football career. Only a few yards, he knew he could do it.

Bruce stood to run and Paul dropped him easily with one shot. He casually strolled past the three bodies, just short of the road. He crossed the rows of corn, remaining hidden from the view of drivers passing by, to retrieve his own hidden pickup. By the time he reached it, darkness had fallen over the cornfield. He eased his pickup slowly down the road, no need for his headlights to attract attention; the full moon sufficiently cast a blue glow over the landscape.

He parked next to the shiny, red Escalade and methodically carried the three bodies to the bed of his vehicle. Always prepared, he carried a blanket behind the seat, along with a flashlight, a small, flat toolbox under the seat, a roll of paper towels and a few chocolate bars in

17

the event he'd become stranded along the side of the road and had to either walk for help or wait patiently for a neighbor to drive by. After tossing a blanket over the bodies, he then broke open one of the hay bales he carried in the back of his truck during cold weather to use for traction if need be. Sprinkling the hay over the blanket, he completely and thoroughly covered his kill.

Slowly, he drove along, fidgeting with his radio for a song that pleased him. He met several neighbors who honked or waved. One stopped him.

"Hi Paul. What's up?"

"Thought I'd do a little hunting."

"Did you get any birds?"

"Nope, not a one. I must be losing my touch."

The two vehicles parted ways. Paul drove to the back of his barn where he ground silage for his cattle. In the darkness of early evening, the full moon continued to assist him. He started his tractor and, using the front-end loader, he picked up a two thousand pound round bale of hay, dropping it into the large flail chopper. The tall, round canister contained blades that spun loosely, chopping any contents into tiny bits. Next, he cut the clothing from his three victims, loaded their bodies into the bucket of the tractor and raised them carefully over the open top of the chopper. Tipping the bucket, they dropped quietly into the hay. While the mixture churned, he stepped just inside his barn and returned with a grain bag. He shoved their clothes inside then tossed them into his burn barrel in the backyard, lighting the contents with the matches he always carried in his pocket. A bit of a firebug, he burned trash and branches daily—partly because he liked to keep the area around his property clean and tidy, and partly because he liked the sight, sound, and smell of fire.

He carefully backed his pickup under the conveyer spout of the chopper, catching the contents as it poured into the bed. The sound of his pickup entering the pasture caused the always-hungry cattle to appear out of the darkness. He stepped out of the pickup while the engine remained running, and it cruised at a slow speed of five miles an hour through the pasture while Paul climbed into the back and shoveled the contents onto the ground, as he did every time he fed the cattle. Sweeping the last bit out of the bed, he jumped down and ran alongside his pickup and climbed in.

He whistled his no particular melody whistle as he pulled into the driveway of his home. He pressed the garage door opener then parked inside. As the door closed, he stomped his feet and brushed the bits of feed from his clothing.

Inside, Liz met him at the door.

"Where've you been?"

"Doin' chores and feeding the cattle. What's for supper?"

"That's it? What's for supper? I told you about those men and you just walked out of here like nothing happened. I can't believe you. Don't you have any compassion at all? What kind of man would allow those guys to get away with what they did?"

Without an answer, he went into the bathroom to wash his hands and face for dinner.

Peggy joined her mother in the kitchen.

"I can't believe it. He just acts like nothing happened," said Liz.

"Mom, what did you expect him to do? I heard everything you told him. I can't believe you made up that story about those men assaulting us in the first place. He must've known you were lying."

Additional Books

by

Patricia A. Bremmer

Titles in the Elusive Clue Series

Tryst With Dolphins

Dolphins' Echo

Death Foreshadowed

Victim Wanted: Must Have References

Crystal Widow

Clinical Death

Mind Your Manors!

Murder's A Cinch

The Christmas Westie

(a children's picture book)

Secret of Dragonfly Island

(a middle grade mysterious adventure)

Legend of Arterburn Lake

(a middle grade mysterious adventure)